THE JOLLY BLOODBATH

The Brothers Quinn

PHOENIX PRESS LTD

Published 2022
First Edition
PHOENIX PRESS LTD
A New Haven Publishing imprint
www.newhavenpublishingltd.com
phoenixpressltd@gmail.com

Cover Design © Pete Cunliffe

PHOENIX
— PRESS —

Content

CHAPTER THE FIRST
BLOOD AND THUNDER

Pirates! The very word still sends shivers down the spine of all decent people. Buccaneers; outlawed wild men and women of the sea, sailing under the black flag of the skull and crossbones, bringing terror to all who crossed their path. Blackbeard, Morgan and Kidd, merciless freebooters whose names will never be forgotten. But there was one pirate so terrible that mankind has purged his memory from existence to save future generations from being driven mad by the horror of his diabolical deeds. So if you are of a nervous disposition be prepared to lose all reason as you travel back to a glorious early spring day in February 1755, to meet Captain Murderer.

***

"It's on days like this that you truly see what a wonderful world we are living in," sighed the Mother Superior of Bilge-on-Sea's Ursuline Convent. Sitting back in the rowing boat as two of her novice nuns struggled with the oars, Mother Superior pushed her wimple back on her forehead to make the most of the sunshine as they scudded across the bay.

"Is this far enough?" panted Sister Dorothy as the boat bobbed up and down on the incoming tide.

"I think so," said Mother Superior. "Open up the picnic basket, girls."

Sisters Dorothy and Ethelreda set a large basket between them and pulled out bread and a large chunk of yellow cheese. As they cut into the cheese a shadow fell over the rowing boat completely blocking out the warm sunshine.

"Belay there!" roared a coarse voice, from above.

All three nuns dropped their bread and cheese in surprise. *The Jolly Bloodbath*, a magnificent galleon, had sailed from nowhere to tower above the rowing boat. A jet black flag emblazoned with a leering skull and crossbones flapped in the rigging, while a pirate with an explosion of red hair and beard bawled at the nuns as he leant over a highly polished cannon.

"Belay there, I say," he repeated. "In the name of Captain Murderer!"

The captain wore a long red frock coat. Actually the coat was made of white linen but had been stained scarlet in all the battles its owner had taken part in. The crew of the ship, an evil, snarling, bunch of cutthroats, glared down at the three women.

"What is it you want?" enquired the Mother Superior, politely. "You are welcome to share our bread and cheese. That's all we have. We belong to a pauper convent."

"No money, eh? That's too bad," bellowed Captain Murderer. "Now I must take my pleasure in another way. Open fire, boys!"

The only good thing that can be said about the following moments is that the nuns didn't know what hit them. But for the sake of our more bloodthirsty readers we can reveal that fifty cannonballs fired at point blank range left only smoke and splinters floating in the water where the little rowing boat had been. Alas, this was not sufficient for Captain Murderer. Wiping gore from his face, his eyes gleamed with bloodlust.

"Prepare for boarding!" he ordered.

"But Captainsss," hissed Hiss, the cabin thing, a shambling, slobbering mess of a man, and servant to the pirate chief. "But, Captainsss, there'sss nothingsss left to board."

"Whaaaatttt?!" screamed Murderer, pulling his cutlass from its scabbard. "Is this mutiny I smell?"

Hiss knew from past experience that this was not a time for explanations. Leaping across the heads of the crew he scrambled up the main mast to hide himself in the crow's nest. He was just in time, for the next moment the captain leapt into the midst of his crew, sword flashing in a berserker's frenzy. They were all tough men but they didn't stand a chance against Captain Murderer with the bloodlust upon him. In less than five minutes not a single one retained a head upon his shoulders. Knee deep in headless pirates the captain waved his stained cutlass at the sky in exhilaration as blood flowed across the deck to gurgle and splatter down the hatches and gangways.

"Victory for Mrs. Murderer's little boy!" he cried.

"Well done, Captainsss," ventured Hiss, peering down from his vantage point high above the deck. He knew that on such occasions a little praise went a long way with his master. The next moment Hiss was thrown from his perch as, with a horrible tearing and grinding, the ship docked by ploughing into the Bilge-on-Sea quayside.

Picking themselves up from the sticky deck the captain and his servant lowered the gangplank and headed into the town, in search of a new crew.

CHAPTER THE SECOND
WELCOME TO BRAKEM ACADEMY

The prospectus for Brakem Academy described the establishment as *being delightfully situated above the town of Bilge-on-Sea*. Eight year old Beatrice Bollingbrook-Drivelington couldn't see anything remotely delightful about the place as her carriage pulled to a halt at the school gates. A dark, gloomy crumbling old pile on a high crag, the starkness of the building was only relieved slightly by the splatter effect of a hundred and fifty years' worth of seagull droppings that covered the walls, roof and grounds, along with a few outcrops of weather-beaten gorse and stunted shrubs growing between the overcrowded tombstones of the school graveyard.

"What a delightful place," said Beatrice's father lifting her down from the carriage. "Just like home!" He was trying to be jolly and drone out the sound of his wife's sobbing from inside the carriage. "I'm sure the years will just fly by in a place like this. Before you know it you will be turning fifteen and returning home to get married." The sobbing turned to a mournful wailing at this revelation so the father pulled his child swiftly into the graveyard. "Let's see who can find the oldest headstone," he beamed. Try as they might the pair could only find stones engraved with dates from the last five years. They came upon a man frantically filling in a new grave with a huge shovel. Mr. Bollingbrook-Drivelington coughed politely and the man spun round at the sound. Beatrice screamed in fear at sight of the fierce yellow tusks that jutted up from his unshaven jaw. His bald head had an angry scar that ran from crown to ear, making it look like a particularly unappetising cracked egg. Beatrice had heard tales of creatures like this. *Angry* seemed to sum up this fierce ogre of a being as he waved the muddy spade threateningly over their heads.

"What do you want?" he demanded. "Off the private property! Off with you now."

"We-we're the Bollingbrook-Drivelingtons," stuttered Beatrice's father. "We're looking for Dr. Bruit, the proprietor of Brakem Academy."

"That's me," said the man, still eyeing them with suspicion. "I've been headmaster here these past five years. Is this the sprog you're leaving? Where's the school fees?"

The doting parent handed over a thick wad of banknotes which seemed to appease the good doctor a little.

"Very nice," he said taking Beatrice's hand roughly. "Don't worry, sir. Brakem Academy will make a man of her. See you in seven years." With that he led Beatrice inside the school building. As their carriage drove away from the school, Beatrice's father decided against telling his distraught wife that their daughter would be a man when next they saw her.

***

As soon as the Bollingbrook-Drivelingtons had vanished over the horizon, Dr. Bruit dragged little Beatrice back out of the school.

"Time for your first lesson, whelp," he growled leading her back to the graveyard. "It's simple arithmetic. Find out how long it would take an eight year old girl to dig a grave six feet deep and three feet wide."

"Can I have a slate to work on?" asked Beatrice, her voice little more than a whisper.

"You don't need a slate," snarled Dr Bruit. "Take this and get digging." He thrust the huge shovel into Beatrice's dainty hands. The shovel was so heavy and the ground was so hard that the answer to the sum was three and a half days. At the end of this time Beatrice's hands were two huge bloody blisters. She staggered into the school and was shown the dormitory by a skinny little boy who introduced himself as Jolly Roger. He seemed to find the funny side of every situation.

"This school is absolutely horrible," he chuckled. "Six pupils have already died this week. Bruit hires us out to do all the ghastly jobs around town. It's a real nightmare, but you've got to laugh, haven't you?"

"Have you?" queried Beatrice lying down on the piece of sackcloth Jolly Roger had pointed out to be her bed.

Two older pupils joined them, dropping down onto their own sackcloth beds. The girl was probably fourteen, and Beatrice thought she was beautiful, in a grubby, under-nourished, wild animal sort of way. Beatrice couldn't help but notice that her arms were covered in garish tattoos of skulls, daggers and other strange symbols.

"I'm Katey, Katey Cross," said the older girl, staring at Beatrice with interest. "Who're you?"

"I'm Beatrice Bollingbrook-Drivelington," said Beatrice, sitting up and offering her hand to Katey. "I'm eight and three quarters."

Katey took her hand and then dropped it quickly in surprise when the little girl screamed and burst into tears.

"Oh, sorry. I suppose you've been on grave digging duty. He always gets the new bugs to do that on their first day. How are the blisters?"

Beatrice sobbed and showed Katey her ruined hands. They looked like something Dr. Bruit might offer one of his hounds for dinner. "Ooh. Nasty. Roger, go and get some bandages will you?"

"Bandages? We ain't got any, we're not a hospital," laughed Roger. He tore the sleeve off his shirt and handed it to Katey. "Here you go," he spluttered. "Oh, I suppose you'll need the other sleeve too. I'll probably freeze to death, but never mind, beats dying of old age, don't it?" He seemed to find this thought so funny that his face turned purple and tears rolled down his cheeks.

"Thank you, Roger," said Beatrice. "You're very kind."

This set him off laughing again. Katey rolled her eyes. "Just ignore him." She turned to the older boy who had come in with her. He was asleep now on his sack cloth bed, snoring lightly. Katey shook him roughly. "Hey, ain't you got no manners? Say hello to the new kid. I forget her name but she's eight and three quarters."

"It's Beatrice Bollingbrook-Drivelington," said Beatrice, staring into one of the bluest eyes she had ever seen.

"Pleased to meetcha," said the owner of that eye, sitting up and treating her to a dazzling smile. He adjusted the grimy patch that covered the place where his other eye should have been and then smiled at her again. "I'm Sam. Sam Skulley, and I'm fifteen and two fifths."

Roger seemed to find Sam's comment hilarious. He doubled over, slapping his thighs and rubbing his sides. "Oh, no," he cried at length, gasping for breath. "I think I've wet myself." He roared out loud again. "Oh well, better out than in."

As Sam and Katey joined in the laughter, Beatrice couldn't help herself, she began to weep and wail. "I'm sorry. I... I'm sure you're all very nice, but I hate this place. I... I want to go home."

Katey gave the little girl a hug. "Shh. It'll be okay. We'll look after you. And one day, we're going to break out of this dump and we'll take you with us."

"Katey, you shouldn't get the girl's hopes up," said Sam, all serious now. "You know it's impossible. The idiots down in Bilge-on-Sea would just send us back and if we tried to escape across the moors, Bruit would send his pack of hounds after us. We'd be torn apart." He ran a grimy hand through his dirty blond hair, dislodging his pig tail and letting it fall down to his shoulders. "The last time I tried to escape Bruit took my eye. I'm not in a hurry to lose the other one."

"There's got to be a way to escape," said Katey, hugging Beatrice close to her. "Don't you worry girl. We'll find it."

"That's right," giggled Roger. "There's always the graveyard. We'll all escape here one day. Hee-hee-hee... Feet first! Bwah-ha-ha!"

CHAPTER THE THIRD
A FEAST FIT FOR A KING

A bell clanged solemnly from somewhere below the dormitory. Sam and Katey pulled Beatrice to her feet. "Come on, you'll be for it if you're late," said Sam.

"Isn't it bedtime yet?" asked Beatrice. She didn't know what time it was but with the moon high in the sky, she was sure it was too late for lessons.

"Lessons?" Katey snorted with contempt. "The only lesson Dr. Bruit teaches us is that life isn't fair. It's dinner time. He always assigns us tomorrow's jobs over dinner, just so he can spoil our appetites."

"Jobs?" said Beatrice, hurrying after the other pupils. "What kind of jobs?"

"The kind no one else in Bilge-on-Sea wants to do," said Sam. "Bruit hires us out to the highest bidders. Today I had to scrub out the town's main sewer pipe. Katey was sweeping chimneys and Roger was...."

"Oh, I was lucky," chortled Roger. "I was helping out as a taster at the local poison manufacturers. They coat some of 'em in chocolate. Lovely stuff, even if it does give you the runs. I keep on tellin' meself, at least I won't die hungry."

"But are you sure you're okay?" asked Beatrice, her eyes wide with worry.

"Don't you worry about him," said Katey. "His belly's made of cast iron. It'd take more than a bit of poison to finish him off."

At last they emerged into a large, smoky hall. A few warped trestle tables lined the walls and bones carpeted the floor. Beatrice noted there were a good two dozen other children already sat at the tables, helping themselves to bowls of what looked like dirty water.

"Hurry up, laggards," snarled the headmaster, who was warming himself beside the open fire, and in the process blocking any heat from reaching the other occupants of the hall. "Eat your water while it's still warm."

Sam, Katey and Roger helped themselves to bowls of water and sat down next to two big and dopey looking twins who introduced themselves as Ronnie and Reggie.

"Wotcha, gel," said Ronnie.

"Keep your eyes off her, I saw her first," said Reggie. Then he elbowed Beatrice in the ribs and laughed. "Only kidding, Duchess."

"Silence!" boomed Dr. Bruit, settling himself down at a separate table next to the fire. He did not share in his pupils' repast, instead, he made do with a seven course meal which included quail's eggs, plover's eggs, roast mutton, roast beef, a joint of lamb, dumplings and chocolate cake. He noticed the children staring at his table with envious eyes and chuckled to himself. "You can look, but you can't touch. This food is far too rich for your delicate constitutions. You'd only make yourselves sick. *Bon appetite*, urchins. That's French. Say it after me, *bon appetite*."

"*Bon appetite*," chorused the hungry children.

"I thankee. Now, who can tell me what *bon appetite* means?" He gazed around the room, ignoring Beatrice

Bollingbrook-Drivelington as she raised her hand and bobbed excitedly up and down on the end of her bench. His cruel eyes turned to a tall African boy, who seemed to be doing his best to avoid notice by slowly sinking beneath the table. "You, what's yer name, boy?"

"Davy, sir. Davy Jones," said the boy, his voice little more than a whisper.

"Well? What's it mean? Astonish us all by your grasp of the French tongue. What does *Bon Appetite* mean?"

"I... I don't know, sir," said Davy trembling with what may have been cold, or quite possibly fear of disappointing his esteemed educator.

Dr. Bruit's bushy eyebrows furrowed across his huge forehead and his jowls took on a purple hue. "Correct. You're a credit to the school, boy. *Bon Appetite* is French for I don't know, and it's the custom to say it before a meal, because people don't know if they're gonna enjoy it or not. Here endeth the lesson." He popped an egg in his mouth and swallowed it whole.

As the good doctor was about to sample his second egg, a loud booming echoed throughout the dining hall. "Hell's teeth, can a man not eat in peace?" he growled, wiping his mouth on the sleeve of his jacket as he rose from the table. "I'll be right back." As the booming continued he stomped out of the hall towards the front door bellowing at the top of his voice. "I'm coming, blast your eyes."

Dr. Bruit had no sooner left the room when Beatrice, whose empty belly could not remember the last time it had been visited by anything more substantial than dirty water, raced forward and snatched the leg of lamb from the headmaster's plate.

"No!" cried Sam Skulley. "Are you mad? He'll kill you!" He tried to pull the girl back to her seat, but not before she had gnawed the meat down to the bone.

"What are we going to do now?" said Sam, staring at the bone in horror. "He'll go crazy when he sees what she's done."

"Keep your milk fresh, Sam," said Ronnie, the twin. "No one's gonna hurt my little princess. Ain't that right, Reg?"

Reggie nodded his head. "Yeah." The twins were on their feet and helping themselves to the food on Bruit's table.

"Everyone's gone mental," laughed Jolly Roger. "We'll be digging fresh graves for breakfast."

The twins were tall for their age and starvation had done little to lessen their appetite for fine meat and eggs. Within the blink of an eye, the plates were clean with just a couple of bones and two Brussels sprouts left untouched.

Reggie eyed the sprouts for a second before popping them in his mouth. "Waste not want not, eh, Ron?" He grimaced at the taste and then belched. "Ahhh, that's better. Right you lot, we're off! Come on Ron." With that, the twins threw themselves through the double windows and raced away into the darkness.

CHAPTER THE FOURTH
BROTHERLY LOVE

While Ronnie and Reggie were eating the headmaster's evening meal, Dr. Bruit was busy fumbling with the locks and chains on the front door. At length he opened it to see his long-lost brother, Captain Murderer, the pirate chief, and Hiss the pirate thing, standing impatiently on the threshold.

"Brother," said the pirate, glaring at the doctor. "You've gotten fat."

"And you've gotten uglier," growled Bruit, snarling with something approaching affection at his little brother.

Now, no doubt gentle reader, you are feeling perhaps a little puzzled. Perhaps you are asking yourself how it could be that a respected headmaster of such a worthy institution as Brakem Academy could be related to such a fiendish and treacherous pirate? How could it be that the two brothers have different surnames? The answer to that is simple. Dr. Bruit, upon installing himself as the proprietor of Brakem Academy feared that the family name *Murderer* would fail to appeal to the parents of his prospective students, therefore he changed it to the softer and more homely Bruit, which was in fact his mother's maiden name. However, it has to be said, that Bruit remained a true Murderer at heart.

"And what ill wind brings you to my door?" asked the doctor, regarding his visitors, with savage curiosity.

"We was in the neighbourhood, looking for a new crew," said Murderer. "And I says to myself, if Bertie knew I was hereabouts and that I never showed my face, he'd never forgive me."

Bertie Bruit sighed. "I could've lived with the disappointment, I assure you. Now, I was just suppin'. You'll join me?"

Murderer clapped his brother hard around the shoulders. "I thought you'd never ask. I'm famished."

"Me too, Captainssss," hissed Hiss, bobbing up and down in excitement.

"You can eat outside in the kennels with the hounds," snapped Bruit and with a rare show of concern for his students, he added, "I don't want you giving the kiddies nightmares."

Murderer kicked the hapless Hiss back into the courtyard and followed his brother into the dining hall. "Ah, but it's good to see you again, Bertie. Your pleasant face always reminds me of our dear sweet Mama, God rest her soul."

"Nooooooooo!" screamed Dr. Bruit, upon entering the hallway and seeing the scant remains of his meal. "Who dares? Who committed this outrage? I'll skin 'em alive. I'll boil them in jam. I'll rip 'em to pieces. I'll play hockey with their shin bones. I'll..."

The children quailed in their seats, all eyes on the floor beneath them. Bruit stared around him and then at the broken window. "The twins. The wretched, stinking, twins. I takes them in, I educates them. I clothes them and they robs me of my victuals and breaks my windows. Is this how they repay my kindness?"

Captain Murderer placed a hand on his brother's shoulder. "They say it is an ill wind that blows no good," he said, a glint in his eye.

"Who says?" asked Bruit, irritably.

"They do. The people who say all the sayings. And they're right. It has been a long time since I felt a good strong stallion between my thighs."

"Eh?" Bruit turned his eyes upon his brother. "Have you taken leave of your senses? I want to eat, not to ride."

"And eat we shall, but first some sport to give the appetite an edge. Call out the hounds. We're going to catch us a couple of foxes."

Bruit thought for a moment and then threw back his enormous head and bellowed with laughter. "A capital idea, Henry." He turned to Davey Jones. "You, saddle my mare and a horse for my brother." He turned to Sam Skulley. "You, look lively, fetch the hounds."

***

Within minutes, Sam, Davey, Katey, Beatrice, Roger and the others were gathered beside the broken window, staring out as Dr. Bruit and Captain Murderer galloped across the graveyard, a pack of baying hounds spreading out before them. The moon was bright but there was no sign of Ronnie or Reggie.

Beatrice began to cry. "It's all my fault. If I hadn't eaten the doctor's food they would never have ..."

"Shhh," said Katey. "It's okay. It'll be okay. Ronnie and Reggie are strong. If anyone could get away from here, it's those two."

19

Jolly Roger began to chuckle softly. "Nothing's faster than those hell hounds. Bruit'll be eating twin pie for his supper before too long. I'd bet your life on it."

The children never did find out for sure what happened to Ronnie and Reggie that night, but the following morning, Katey Cross and Beatrice Bollingbrook-Drivelington noticed Bruit's hounds paying frenzied attention to two piles of bones that they were dragging around the school grounds.

"Is that...?" began Beatrice, sobbing with horror.

"No," said Katey, biting her lip. "The dogs have probably been digging in the graveyard, that's all. They're forever digging someone up. Don't worry about it."

CHAPTER THE FIFTH
A SCHOOL OUTING

After a breakfast of crumbs and nettles, washed down with water freshly pumped from the cesspit, the children of Brakem Academy were getting ready to depart for their morning's chores, Roger to the poison factory, Katey to the Sewage Corporation and Sam to the bone grinder's yard, when Dr. Bruit and his brother came out to inspect them. Neither of these two worthies could be described as morning people and on this particular morning both of them were recovering from the excesses of the night before. Their eyes were red and their heads heavy.

"Right you maggots, you're all coming with us today," said Bruit, his voice quieter than normal. "A school outing. We're going to learn all about woodwork and carpentry."

"Oh, goody," said Beatrice, clapping her hands together. "I want to make a doll's house. My daddy gave me one for my sixth birthday but he wouldn't let me bring it here."

"Shut your great big cakehole!" roared Bruit. "Do you think we want to listen to your senseless chattering?"

Beatrice shook her head and stared at her feet, doing her best not to cry and failing miserably. "Sorry, sir."

Captain Murderer put his arm around his brother's shoulder and gave him an affectionate hug. "You're a saint, lad, a real saint. Takin' the trouble you do with these miserable whelps. If it was up to me, I'd skin 'em alive, turn 'em inside out and hang 'em out to dry by their fingernails."

Bruit sighed like a martyr. "Aye well, that's coz you never had the calling like me. When I saw how much their parents were willin' to pay me just to take the little blisters off their hands, I knew teachin' was the life for me. A sacred duty so to speak."

The two men climbed aboard the carriage Hiss had prepared for them. Bruit stuck his head out of the window and told the pupils to run ahead of them. "If any of you slows down, we'll grind your bones to dust."

And so it was that the pupils of Brakem Academy raced the three and three quarter miles to the harbour at Bilge-on-Sea, where the *Jolly Bloodbath* lay at anchor. The run had been bracing for all concerned, resulting in only two casualties, a young lad from Halifax whose name nobody could remember, and a girl called Hettie who had also been too slow to get out of the way of Bruit's carriage. The accident had been a stroke of luck for the rest of the pupils who had been allowed five minutes rest while Hiss scraped their flattened remains from the road and placed them in a barrel for pickling.

The sight of the *Jolly Bloodbath* filled most of the pupils of the Academy with dread. It was an evil ship, huge, fearsome and foul smelling. A cloud of flies buzzed across the decks, attracted by the spilt blood and the remains of Captain Murderer's crew. Katey Cross, however, was not afraid. She stared at the ship in wonder and admiration.

"It's beautiful," she whispered.

"You want your eyes tested," said Sam.

"Right you lot, study time," said Bruit, standing on the gangplank. "As I promised, today's workshop is woodwork. We're startin' at the beginning and we're gonna show you how to care for wood. So, get swabbin' the decks!"

As the children stumbled aboard the ship, Hiss handed each one a scrubbing brush and a bucket of water. Captain Murderer approached him. "Hiss, me an' my brother have business to discuss in town. Keep an eye on this lot an' don't be afraid to kill 'em if they step out of line."

"Trusssst me, Masterssss," slobbered Hiss, giving Davey Jones a kick in the behind, to show he was up for the task.

"Come on, brother," cried the Captain. "Drinkin' time's a wasting."

***

It was hard work for the pupils because it was a very big ship and it was very, very dirty. It didn't help things that every so often a decapitated pirate's head would roll out from behind a barrel or from under a coil of rope. As she scrubbed at yet another stubborn, sticky, red stain on the main deck, Katey caught Sam's eye and nodded for him to join her.

"This could be our way out of here," she whispered as they scrubbed away.

"What do you mean?" asked Sam.

"The ship," Katey explained. "We could escape on the ship."

"You must be joking! Murderer would sling us overboard as soon as he found us."

"I know. That's why we're going to take the ship ourselves before he sails away."

"Only one small problem with that," said Sam. "We haven't a clue how to sail a ship."

"I know, but he does!" Katey whispered, dodging aside as Hiss hurled a barrel of rum at her.

"Get sssscrubbing or I'll tell masterssss," he slobbered.

***

On the way back to the school that night, Sam jogged alongside Katey.

"Do you really think we could do it?" he asked.

"Probably not," she answered. "But it suits me better than waiting to take my place in the school graveyard.

CHAPTER THE SIXTH
THE GREAT ESCAPE

That night, Dr. Bruit and Captain Murderer threw a banquet at Brakem Academy. The guests of honour were the new crew members they had successfully recruited from the taverns of Bilge-on-Sea. Captain Murderer prided himself on never press-ganging crew members for service on the *Jolly Bloodbath*. "Every man who sails on her, sails of his own free will, in the hopes of drowning in more treasure than he can dream of," he would boast to all who cared to listen. "If they don't wanna come, then may the devil take 'em." As a rule, when faced with the choice of service on the most successful pirate ship of the age, or being skewered on the end of a rusty cutlass, most people opted for a life of piracy.

Now, the *Bloodbath* could be at sea for many months at a time, therefore, whenever recruiting a new crew, it was customary for Captain Murderer to invite the sailors to a banquet in order to get to know them better. If any of them failed to impress, or proved dull and boring, or could not sing his favourite sea shanties, then they would invariably find themselves headless, legless and armless before the night was done. "It's just my way of separatin' the wheat from the chaff, the men from the boys and the wood from the trees," he would explain. Most people found the process sensible enough, and those who didn't seldom found themselves in a position to complain.

Dr. Bruit enjoyed hosting the banquet. Even his fiercest critics would often note that, say what you like against the headmaster, one thing was certain, he knew how to throw a good party. A schoolmaster's life is often lonely, and he seldom got to mix in adult company. Whenever the chance came along he was determined not to be found wanting. He pressed the pupils into service, utilizing Sam Skulley as head waiter, Katey Cross as head chef and the others as maids and footmen.

The evening's festivities passed off without a hitch, and without any fatalities, except for the death of two prospective pirates who Captain Murderer beheaded by accident whilst carving the meat.

At length, after several long and exhausting toasts to 'death and damnation', the pirates had all passed out and the children were left to clear up the mess.

"I'm bushed," sighed Sam, stretching. "I could sleep for a thousand years."

"Sleep's for losers, Sam," said Katey, coming out from the kitchen, her face red and sweating from the heat of the ovens. "There's a fine breeze blowing up outside and Bruit and his horrible brother are completely out of it."

"So?" Sam knew where this was going but he didn't like it. He didn't like it at all.

"If we go tonight, we'll have the wind in our sails. We'll be halfway to where ever we're going before morning." She turned to the exhausted children that had gathered around her. "Who's up for a midnight cruise?"

Every hand shot up, except for Sam's. He looked at the hopeful faces and wondered how many of them would survive Katey's planned excursion. Then he realized that he could not remember the last time anyone had looked anywhere remotely hopeful. Wasn't it better to die with hope than to survive without it? He bit his lip and nodded his head. "Very well. Bruit's got the front door keys anyone want to try and pick his pockets?"

"No," said Katey. "Too risky. Come on, I've got an idea."

The children followed her into the dormitory where she began tying their sackcloth bedding together in rough seaman's knots. "Come on, we'll make a rope. Look lively, we're breaking out."

Everyone worked together, as one, now that they had made the decision they had to execute the plan before the pirates awoke. Within minutes they had fashioned a rope long enough, they hoped, to reach from the parapet to the rocky ground below.

"You go first," said Sam, nodding at Katey. "It's your idea. You should be the first to escape."

"You mean I should be the one to check if this is strong enough to hold our weight," she said with a grin. "Okay, in that case, you go last, that way you can help anyone who gets into trouble."

Sam agreed, although he was unsure just how he would be able to help anyone who got into trouble on the long climb down. He tied one end of the rope to the flagpole attached to the parapet and gave it a good tug. The flagpole bent slightly with the strain. "I don't know if this is strong enough but it's all we have. You ready?"

Katey was nervous. Heights had never been her strong point, but she knew the others were relying on her. They needed her to be strong and fearless. Without a word, she took the rope from Sam and tossed it over the wall. Then she began the descent. No sooner had she began lowering herself down than the wind began to buffet her. It was almost as if the elements themselves had joined forces with Dr. Bruit and were determined to halt the escape. "Nonsense," she told herself. Down and down she went, ignoring the pain as the rope dug into the palms of her hands. At the halfway point, she no longer had any feeling in her arms. She wanted to rest against the granite gargoyle but she knew that if she stopped for an instant she would never find the strength to continue. "The climb didn't look so bad from the top," she thought to herself. "Now it seems endless." Then, just as the need to rest became all consuming, a bat skimmed past the top of her head, making her cry out. She let go of the rope and fell.

Luckily, the drop was less than a couple of feet and she landed on her feet, not exactly like a cat, but at least she was still in one piece and apart from the pain in her hands and the ache in her shoulders, she was unhurt. She drew in a deep breath and let out a noise like an owl.

"Katey?" Sam called down to her, his voice echoing off the walls of the Academy.

"Shhh!" she hissed. But he couldn't hear her.

"Katey?" he yelled, louder this time.

"Shutup, you idiot! I'm fine. Why do you think I gave the owl signal?"

Sam peered down over the parapet. He couldn't see her but she could see him, the moon full and bright behind him. "Was that you? I thought it was an owl. Right, I'll send the next one down."

Jolly Roger came next, chuckling and laughing all the way down. The others followed in quick succession until at last all that remained were Sam Skulley and Beatrice Bollingbrook-Drivelington.

"Right, you ready?" Sam asked her.

Beatrice fought back the tears and shook her head. "I can't do it. I'm not strong enough."

"Course you are."

"I'm not. I'm scared. I won't do it."

"We can't go without you."

"You could carry me?"

Sam cursed inwardly. "Carry you?" Certainly, Beatrice was small, but it was a long climb and any extra weight was bad news, but he had no choice. Dawn was less than an hour away. "Come on then. Climb up and hang on tight." She climbed onto his back and hung tight to his neck. "Hold onto my shoulders, not my neck. You're strangling me."

At last they were ready and he lowered himself over the edge of the parapet and began his descent. It was raining now and the walls were slippery against his feet. Halfway down and he felt the rope moving dangerously. The flagpole was beginning to break. He doubled his speed. Then he felt hands reaching up and taking Beatrice from his shoulders. He had made it. They had made it, with no fatalities, no injuries. Beatrice stood on tip-toe and kissed his sweaty cheek.

"Thank you," she said, quietly.

"You're welcome. Come on, let's go."

They crawled on all fours past the windows of the great hall and then crossed the graveyard as they set off in the direction of the harbour. The wind, which had grown even stronger, seemed to blow them at top speed towards the *Jolly Bloodbath* as it bobbed and rocked wildly at the quayside. Crossing the gangplank, they made a quick search of the ship. Hiss was the only pirate on board. He was supposed to be on watch duty, but he had taken advantage of the captain's absence to catch up on his ugly sleep instead. Loud snores echoed from his lair deep in the fetid hold.

"Lock him in," ordered Katey. "He can help us once we're out at sea. Now cast off all the ties to the quay and let's raise the anchor."

It took the strength of all the children to haul the heavy anchor back up onto the ship.

"Just one more thing and we're ready to sail," said Sam. Snatching a frightening looking sword from the deck he began to climb up the mast towards the mainsail. It was a difficult climb with the wind, rain and lurching of the ship but at last he stood atop the carefully folded sail. With two slashes of the sword he cut the ties binding the sail which unfolded to the deck where Katey instructed the kids to tie it off with the firmest of knots.

Sam clung for his life onto the mast as the sail flooded with the gale-force wind, shooting the ship like a bullet away from the quayside. "We're freeeeee!" he roared.

***

Captain Algernon Righteous, was the poster boy of the British Navy. Young, dashing, of noble birth, and as virtuous and pure as the day is long, he was the stuff that legends are made of. He smiled through the wind and the rain as he expertly spun the wheel of the *HMS Camilla* to guide it through the heart of the storm towards Bilge-on-Sea. The ship was the flagship of the Royal Navy, and Righteous had been awarded its captaincy that very day by King George himself. For its maiden voyage he had taken the king on a day trip to Calais. They were halfway across the Channel when the storm blew up out of nowhere. Righteous was not unduly bothered. They were due to dock at Southampton, but the storm would allow him a few more hours in the company of his liege and monarch. He decided to take refuge in the harbour at Bilge-on-Sea until the storm blew over.

He was thinking about how he could entertain the King with tales of his adventures in the New World over supper. He could also impress him with his new knowledge of the German language, which he had been practicing daily for weeks in the privacy of his cabin. "Old George's English isn't quite up to scratch, I bet he'll love the chance of a good old chinwag in German," Righteous thought to himself. His smile turned to a frown as he noticed a shape looming up out of the darkness. His frown turned to a scream as the *Jolly Bloodbath* bore down on him at top speed. It was all over in a blink of an eye. There was a terrible rending and splintering of wood as Righteous was thrown off his feet. He just had time to see the name *The Jolly Bloodbath*, emblazoned on the figurehead as the pirate ship rocketed by on its journey out to sea. Five minutes later and *HMS Camilla* was sinking to the floor of the English Channel as Captain Algernon Righteous and King George in his nightdress floundered desperately through the choppy waters towards Bilge-on-Sea.

CHAPTER THE SEVENTH
RIGHTEOUS INDIGNATION

As soon as they reached land Captain Righteous took off his tunic and hung it around the shoulders of his shivering king. Righteous was chilled to the bone himself but he would sooner die of the ague than permit his liege to catch cold. Sadly, King George, who had awoken to find himself floating in icy water as the pride of his Royal Navy sank beneath him, was not in an appreciative mood.

"Perdition! What are you playing at man?" he flung the sodden coat in the captain's face. "This coat is even wetter than I am. I need drying off, not another soaking! Bring me a towel."

Captain Righteous glanced around the rain-lashed harbour but saw nothing that even faintly resembled a dry towel. He bit his lip and bowed. "Sire, due to the inclement weather conditions and the fact that I too have just recently swam ashore, I am not in possession of a dry towel." The captain then did a most extraordinary thing and advancing upon the King he began rubbing the royal head vigorously with his hands.

"Agghh! Have you gone mad, Righteous? What the devil d'you think you're doing, sir?" cried the King, as his wig came away in the captain's hands.

"Improvising, Sire," replied Righteous, attempting to replace the wig upon his king's head. "If it would only stop raining I would have you dry in a jiffy."

The King's patience was at an end. "Listen to me, Righteous. I am going to the nearest tavern where I shall attempt to do my best to forget all about tonight. You, on the other hand, are going to set about apprehending those pirates that sunk our ship and bringing them to justice. I swear, if they aren't hanging at Tyburn by Ascension Day, you will have to take their place. Now get out of my sight!"

Captain Righteous may have been a fool, but he knew when he was fighting a lost cause, so doing his best not to appear too hurt, he bade his king a fond farewell and set about finding a new ship in which to pursue the *Jolly Bloodbath*.

***

Back at Brakem Academy, Dr. Bruit and Captain Murderer had awoken from their slumbers and were in the mood for fun and mirth.

"Brother," said Bruit. "How do you feel about frightening the kiddies out of their wits?"

"I feel intrigued," said Murderer, draining the dregs from a bottle of rum. "Just how do you propose to do it?"

"Let's dress up in sheets. They'll think we're the ghosts of their classmates come to haunt 'em. It'll be a right laugh."

"I've got a better idea," said Murderer. "Let's shove the little beasts into our empty barrels of rum and roll 'em down the hill into the sea. We can take bets to see whose barrel sinks first."

"Righto," laughed Bruit. "I'm game for anything I am. I'm a right old nutter me. Anything for a laugh."

The pirates scrambled for their pistols and followed the good doctor and their captain to the dormitory.

"Hang me high!" growled Bruit as he entered the room and found his pupils had vanished. "Where are the little maggots?" He cast a suspicious eye at his cousin. "Hey, you ain't pressganged them into service, have you? If you have, I won't stand for it. They're mine, every last one of 'em."

Captain Murderer shook his head. "They've deserted ship, you fool. Come on, let's be after them lads. We'll have fun punishing them for this!"

Dr Bruit fetched his hounds from the stables and the search began. It didn't take long for the dogs to find the scent of the runaways, and so with much baying and howling for blood, the headmaster, his dogs and the pirates took up the chase.

"They're headed down towards the harbour!" Bruit roared over the howling wind.

Captain Murderer's good mood was evaporating in the chill of the wind and the rain. "Hey, we'll stop off at the ship, maybe Hiss has seen them sneaking past."

The dogs, Bruit, Murderer and his crew came to an abrupt halt at the quayside.

"Where's the *Jolly Bloodbath*?" screamed Captain Murderer. "She was here, I know she was. Who has stolen my lovely *Bloodbath*?"

They gazed out to sea but all was dark and grim, it had been a good twenty minutes since the *Bloodbath* vanished over the horizon.

"I reckon them kids must've nicked your boat," giggled one of the newly recruited pirates. "Imagine that, a gang of kids nickin' the great Captain Murderer's boat."

Murderer had heard enough. He drew his cutlass and with one fell swoop, the unfortunate pirate's head was separated from his body and rolling into the sea. "Half wit!" he growled, wiping his sword on his sleeve. "*The Jolly Bloodbath* is a ship, not a boat."

One of the pirates kneeled down by the body of his fallen friend and began to weep. "There was no need to do that, Cap'n. He was a good lad, he was. I've sailed with him for over twenty years. Like a brother he was."

Dr. Bruit sighed. He knew his brother well, and if one thing was likely to annoy him it was people not getting the joke when he had killed someone close to them. He knew it was pointless saying anything, so he merely stepped out of the way and watched, a faint smile on his hideous face.

"A good lad was he?" said Murderer, drawing his pistol and shooting the weeping pirate. "That's what I think of good lads."

"Steady on, Skipper," cried out another. "Calm down, don't let's go over the top."

Murderer threw off his jacket, rolled up his sleeves and set about the business of slaughtering his crew...again. At last, when he was waist-high in gore, he sheathed his cutlass and glared at his brother, who was lurking nervously in the shadows. "This is your fault, Bertie. If it weren't for you and your stupid kids, I'd still have a ship and a crew. Give me one good reason why I shouldn't kill you too."

Bruit thought for a moment and smiled. "I'll help you get your ship back and I'll buy you a bottle of rum at the tavern."

"Make it a barrel of rum and you've got a deal. Killing is thirsty work."

Murderer spat on his hand and offered it to his brother to shake and therefore seal the deal, before the two of them made their way to Dr. Bruit's favourite tavern, the Hanged Man.

***

As the brothers drowned their sorrows in rum in a corner of the Hanged Man, they were so wrapped up in thoughts of revenge upon the children that they didn't notice the four rough looking sailors warming themselves before the open fire.

"I swear, I'm gonna make those kids pay for this," cursed Captain Murderer. "I'm gonna slit 'em open from gizzard to gurney, fill 'em up with pebbles, stitch 'em up again and jiggle them up and down till they're sick."

"Yeah!" agreed Dr. Bruit. "Then I'm gonna hit them with a stick. A big stick."

Captain Murderer nodded his head, seriously. "Mmm. Good idea. The simplest ideas are often the best. You're a good bloke, Bertie. A damn good bloke."

"So are you," said Bruit, wiping a tear from his eye. "Ah, if only our Mammy was here now. What would she think?"

"She'd probably think we was idiots for sitting here drinking when we should be chopping heads," sighed Murderer. "Still, revenge is a dish best served cold, as she liked to say. Now, how're we gonna get hold of a ship to chase after them kids of yours?"

Dr. Bruit never had the chance to answer the question, for at that moment a heavy oak cudgel came crashing down on his head, sending him unconscious to the floor.

Captain Murderer stared in astonishment at the four rough looking sailors who were surrounding him. Then he began to laugh. "Good one, lads. I've wanted to brain him ever since I was six. Did you see the look on his face? Let me get you a drink."

Far from taking the captain up on his generous offer, the four sailors set about him with their cudgels, until he too was stretched unconscious upon the filthy floor of the tavern.

***

Hours later, Captain Murderer and Dr. Bruit awoke to find themselves bound in chains in the hold of a ship. Murderer could tell from the swaying of the floor beneath him that they were already at sea. He was just wondering if he had been recognised and arrested when the hatch above them opened and daylight streamed in. Two sailors climbed down the ladder, unchained them and forced them up on deck. Murderer looked about him and swallowed. He was on the deck of a British man o' war, and facing him was an officer of the British Navy.

The officer smiled at the brothers. "My apologies, gentlemen, for the manner in which you were brought here, but desperate times call for desperate measures. My name is Captain Algernon Righteous and you, sirs, have been press-ganged into the Royal Navy to help in the fight against piracy. It is our duty, gentlemen, to track down the *Jolly Bloodbath* and bring their vile and dastardly crew to justice."

Captain Murderer hated the idea of taking orders from anyone else, but for the moment he decided to play along.

"Very good, sir," he grinned. "'Tis an honour and a privilege to serve alongside you."

"Me too," grunted Dr Bruit. "Hey, have you got anything for headaches? Me bonce is killing me."

CHAPTER THE EIGHTH
ALL AT SEA

The Jolly Bloodbath continued to pick up speed as it smashed through the hull of the *HMS Camilla*. Katey Cross looked around frantically. She had no idea what to do or how to bring the ship under control. Her 'crew' were of no use. Most of them were hiding or being sick, or wailing in terror. Sam Skulley, the one on whom she knew she could count was stuck up the rigging, unable to descend for fear of being blown away to sea. Only Jolly Roger seemed unconcerned, he was roaring with laughter as the rain and wind buffeted him around the deck.

"What a hoot, eh? We risk death climbing down from the school and then we all end up drowned. Life's funny like that, ain't it?"

"Nobody's going to drown," Katey shouted over the wind. "Come on, we need help." Arming herself with a rusty cutlass, she raised the hatch to the hold and beckoned Roger to follow her. Beatrice Bollingbrook-Drivelington followed after and nearly slipped on the blood-soaked steps.

"Easy, girl," laughed Roger, grabbing hold of her. "There's better ways than that to break your neck."

Hiss was awake by now. Awake and bewildered. "Girlsss on ship? Thisss not good. Bad luck. Bad luck. Bad luck. What isss thissss?"

"We're running this ship now," said Katey.

Hiss's eyes filled with tears. "But what about my Captain? Where'ssss my lovely Murderer?"

"Gone," said Katey. "You'll never see him again."

"Noooooo!" Hiss shrieked like a scalded cat and began throwing himself at the walls of the hold before leaping over Roger's head and scampering up the steps to the deck. "Captainssss! I wantsss my Captainssss."

"What'll we do?" asked Beatrice. "He's not going to work for us."

"He will, he has to," said Katey. "We need to scare him. We'll threaten to keel haul him if he doesn't do as he's told."

"Keel haul? What's that?" asked Beatrice.

Katey shrugged. "Dunno. But it must be bad. Pirates are always going on about it. Anyway, it doesn't matter. We're not going to really do it."

"You're going to lie to him?" asked Beatrice. "That's not nice."

Katey shrugged. "Yeah, well. I don't think being nice will get us very far, do you?"

They climbed up on deck. Hiss was cowering beside the ship's wheel, snapping and biting like a dog.

"Stop that," said Katey. "You're going to work for us."

"Never."

"If you don't do as I say, we'll have you keel hauled."

Hiss stared at her in awe and terror. "Keel hauled? No, misstressss. Anything but that. Kill me pleassse but don't keel haul me."

Katey was impressed. "So, you don't want to be keel hauled, eh?"

"No, missstressss. Have mercy. Pleassse."

"And what is it exactly about being keel hauled that you don't like?"

"I don't likesss any of it, missstresssss."

"Yes, but which bit is the worst bit about being keel hauled?" Katey had a thirst for knowledge that had never been quenched by Dr. Bruit.

"The wet bitsss," said Hiss. "The wet bitsss are the worsssst."

Still none the wiser, Katey decided to put her lesson in sailing on hold for a while until they were out of the storm. "Well, we'll keel haul you with all the wet bits if you don't help us sail this ship."

It did the trick. Hiss stood to attention and saluted his new captain. "Where do you wantss to go, mistresss?"

Katey looked at Roger and Beatrice. This was something none of them had thought about. "Where do we want to go?"

Beatrice was the first to speak. "I want to go home. I miss my Mummy and Daddy and Licky."

"Licky?" asked Katey.

"My doggy. You would love him. Mummy and Daddy will know what we should do and you can all come and see my bedroom. It's green."

"I likessss green," said Hiss.

"Very well," said Katey. "Let's go to Beatrice's. Do you know where it is?"

"No," said Beatrice. "It's on the coast somewhere. It's near a place called Bloom."

"That'ssss in Cornwall," said Hiss, turning the ship's wheel. "I likesss Cornwall and green."

"Very well," said Katey, "let's go to Bloom."

CHAPTER THE NINTH
THE SONG OF THE SIREN

Hiss was a good sailor, better than his former master would ever have believed. He negotiated rocks, the storm and managed to lose an approaching vessel which may or may not have been hostile. By mid afternoon they had left the storm behind and were sailing on a calm sea, on their way towards Cornwall.

The 'crew' had all calmed down and were busy cleaning the decks and repairing sails, all under Hiss's orders. When they were done, he set about teaching them all the rude sea shanties in his repertoire as they feasted upon the meat and nuts Davey Jones had found in the store room. Davey Jones and Billy Bones were fine cooks and as the sun began to set a strange feeling came over the escapees. Happiness, a thing none of them had known in a long time. Sadly, as Dr. Bruit always liked to remind them, 'happiness' is fleeting. As the crew sang and ate, the sounds of their merriment travelled across the sea to a small outcrop of rocks, known to all as 'the Devil's Fangs'. The occupants of those rocks raised their ugly, scaly heads and listened. "Food," said one. "Food," chorused the others.

If you were short sighted and without your glasses you could be forgiven for mistaking these creatures for human women, but a closer look, with a decent pair of specs would reveal that these beings were far from human. So hideous were they that they made Hiss look handsome. Their skin was grey, the grey of a dead fish's belly. Scales covered their flesh, and their hair was the black, brown and green of seaweed. Huge clumps of it hung from their armpits and chins. In place of legs they had fish tails, yes, these things were as closely related to the mermaids as we are to the baboon. There was nothing beautiful about the sirens. Even their singing, which legend has it, was so beautiful it would lure unwary seamen to their deaths, was totally overrated. Not one of them could carry a tune, indeed, it is more likely that the sailors chose death by drowning as an escape from the foul, nerve shredding sound of their hideous voices. They sang now on the command of their Queen, the oldest and ugliest of all the sirens. The Queen liked to be referred to as Queenie, she was so old and had been queen for so long she could barely remember her given name and anyway Queenie sounded much grander.

"Let us sing them onto the rocks," she croaked. "Ready, my beauties!"

The 'beauties' began to sing.

On the deck of the *Jolly Bloodbath*, Hiss was leading them in the seventeenth verse of 'Blow the man down'. He danced a little jig, much to the enjoyment of all. Jolly Roger was laughing so hard that nobody heard the strange, unearthly racket that constituted 'singing' for the sirens. Frustrated, they left the Devil's Fangs, and swam closer to the ship.

"They still can't hear us," said one to the Queen.

"Don't worry, my dear," said Queenie. "Louder and with gusto. When they catch sight of me, they will be so entranced by my beauty that they will jump overboard for a kiss."

They sang louder, as they approached the ship under the red rays of the setting sun.

"What's that horrible racket?" asked Davey Jones.

"Hiss singing? It ain't that bad," Billy Bones replied.

"No. Listen."

"*Grind 'em, grind 'em grind 'em...*" came a horrible wail from the sea.

Sam Skulley looked overboard but he could see nothing. "It's horrible, whatever it is."

The singing grew louder. The children stuffed their fingers in their ears and tried not to be sick. Hiss alone appeared enchanted.

"Lovely mussssicsss," he said. "It remindsss me of my Mummy." He stood up and peered down into the water and gasped at the sight of the sirens, swimming around the ship. "Loveliesss, lovely beautiessss."

"Ewww, they're horrible," said Beatrice, looking down. "And they stink."

It may not have been a polite observation, but it was certainly true. A strong aroma of sweat and fish filled the air.

"*Grind them bones dowwwwn...*"

"Shut up!" yelled Katey.

"Louder, girls," said Queenie. "They're falling for it."

The sirens began to wail all the louder. Billy Bones was the first to throw up over the side of the ship, right on top of Queenie.

"Oi!" she yelled. "I'm a Queen, you can't puke on me."

Beatrice was next to throw up. "Oops. Sorry," she called down. "But could you stop that horrible racket? It's making everyone ill."

"Ill?" said Queenie, incredulous. "Nonsense. It is beautiful. You've never heard such beauty and so it is making you sick. It's just like enjoying a plate of octopus guts and sucking on squid teeth. Sometimes the flavour is too much."

"If you don't cut that racket out right now, I'm going to open fire," said Sam, training a cannon down into the water.

"Well of all the impudence," said Queenie. "Let's try harder, girls. Let's sing these rude little pests to their doom."

They began to sing even louder. It was too much for Hiss. "Beautiful ssssingerssss. Hisss wantsss a kisssss." He leaped overboard and the sirens swooped towards him, teeth flashing.

"Din-dins," laughed Queenie.

"They're going to eat him," cried Beatrice.

"No," said Katey. "Nobody eats my crew, not even Hiss. Open fire."

Sam lit the fuse and a cannon ball sped through the sirens scattering them.

"Well," said Queenie. "Of all the nerve."

One of the sirens had taken a bite out of Hiss's toe and he was screaming in pain. She spat the fragment of toenail out in disgust.

"He tastes horrible, Queenie."

"He smells horrible too. Maybe we need one of the fresher ones." Queenie wrapped Hiss up in her tail and tossed him back on board the *Jolly Bloodbath*.

"Noooo!" cried Hiss. "I wanttsss to be with beautiful smelling fish ladiesssss." Katey had to hold him down to stop him from throwing himself back overboard.

"They don't want you, Hiss. Stop it."

"Nobody wantsss me," Hiss sobbed. "Not fishhh ladiesss, not Captainsss Murderer and not youssss."

"I want you, Hiss," said Beatrice, giving him a hug.

Sam had fired another cannonball into the water and now the wind was in their sails once more and the *Jolly Bloodbath* was flying away from the Devil's Fangs and the murderous sirens.

"You haven't heard the last of us," screeched Queenie. "We will eat you, I promise you."

Jolly Roger was beside himself with laughter. "Ha! Imagine that, almost eaten by mythological creatures that don't even exist. Some people have all the luck."

"Land ho!" cried Katey, pointing to an outcrop of cliffs in the distance.

"I know that place," said Beatrice, jumping up and down. "That's my beach. My house is just over the other side of those cliffs. Cheer up, Hiss. You can play with Licky tonight."

"Lucky me," said Hiss, who was still glancing back behind them, hoping for another sight of the creature who had bitten off his toe.

CHAPTER THE TENTH
HOME SWEET HELL

Quite how a bunch of inexperienced kids + a single piratical thing were able to beach a galleon without holing it or at the very least causing extreme damage to its hull is almost beyond belief so we won't waste time describing the actions of the young crew as there is absolutely nothing to be learned from them. We shall just say that it was sheer good luck that allowed Dr. Bruit's former pupils and Hiss to be heading along the cliff path one hour later. Beatrice led the way, skipping, jumping, tripping and laughing as she went.

"That's my favourite view," she squeaked, pointing to a crumbling watchtower that topped the cliff. "And that's my favourite tree. And that's my favourite bush. And that's my favourite boulder. And that's my favourite hedge..."

As the group topped the cliff, the clouds parted and a brilliant sunbeam shone down directly onto Bollingbrook Hall, flickering off the 950 windows on the East side of the grand building. "And that's my favourite house," squealed Beatrice in a key only dogs could hear. It was indeed a beautiful pile but it has been said (by those who say) that beauty is only skin deep, and if young Beatrice could have seen her dear Mother falling from the topmost window on the West side of the house at that precise moment, her home might have dropped to second place in

47

her Top Ten Favourite Houses Chart. We say falling but the sad matter is that she was pushed. Yes, pushed, and by her own husband of ten years (it was in fact their wedding anniversary), Donald Drivelington. You see, Donald had married above his station. The Bollingbrooks were quality people and had been moneyed landowners since the days of good King John while the Drivelingtons had been bankrupts, wastrels and spendthrifts since the Bronze Age. To top it all, Donald was a gambler. The gee-gees, don'tcha know. Just that morning his wife had found the bills. Over 300 of them. He'd tried to explain but she was having none of it. So, on the spur of the moment, he felt he could solve all his problems by throwing her out of the top window. In his favour it has to be said that by the time his wife hit the courtyard below, he was already having second thoughts. He leaned out of the window and looked down at the mess.

"That's going to take some cleaning," he mused. "Lucky there's nobody else at the Hall today, so that should give me time to think." It was at that second that there came the echoing boom of the front door knocker. It gave Donald such a shock that he almost followed his wife out of the window.

By the time he got downstairs he had drenched two man-size handkerchiefs by mopping his fevered brow. Imagine his delight on throwing open the door to find his daughter, classmates and Hiss on the doorstep!

"Daddy! My favourite Daddy!" sobbed Beatrice, rushing into his arms. "Please don't be mad at me for sagging off school. Dr. Bruit was going to kill and eat us all. These are my classmates, except for Hiss who's a pirate. Where's Mummy and Licky?"

A very good question that deserves a sweeter answer than the factual one that Licky was at that moment in the back courtyard living up to his name with the remains of Mummy.

CHAPTER THE ELEVENTH
WET BITS AND SHARP BITS

Back on the high seas, Captain Algernon Righteous's new command, the *HMS Cheryl*, bobbed up and down more than is good for anyone not born the seventh son of the seventh son of a seadog. Luckily there was only one such on board the vessel, but this was a very important one such. The King no less. He had insisted on coming along on this Voyage of Justice as he called it.

"We shall smite off the hands, knees and bumpsadaisies of every villain on *The Jolly Bloodbath*," he swore. "And then we shall - WHURRRP - hang them, while still alive note, outside schools - WHURRRP - and Olde Folks Homes as a - WHURRRP - deterrent to people of all ages. Damnation to them all and to this accursed seasickness - WHURRRP!"

The crew, many of them covered in his accursed seasickness, cheered at this.

"He's a rum 'en, ain't 'e?" remarked Dr. Bruit, nudging his brother, the good Captain Murderer, in the ribs.

"Arrr, not very majestic for a king," replied Murderer. "Fat little toad he be. Can't stand a man who can't keep down his own vomit."

"What's that?" cried the King. He had heard plain enough but couldn't quite believe his ears. Like most kings George was used to lickspittles and crawlers, subjects who recognised him as being only second to God in the magnificent stakes. He walked over to Murderer and stood on tip-toe so he could glare into his eyeballs. "What did you say, man? Come on, spit it out! WHURRRP!" Unfortunately it was the King who spat it out. Semi digested veal, potatoes, cabbage and corn (always the corn) splattered into Captain Murderer's face and ran down his best bib and tucker.

"Uh-oh, now we're in for stormy weather," sighed Bruit. "Batten down the hatches."

Truer words were never spoken. You do not throw up with impunity into the face of a pirate named Murderer and get off scott free. By the time the King hit the deck he had two black eyes, one broken nose, six missing teeth and half his left ear bitten off. It was Captain Righteous himself who stopped the bout by smacking Murderer a mighty blow over the head with his sextant.

"Get this man in chains!" he screamed at his crew. "And fetch the ship's doctor and dentist and carry the King to my cabin!"

Now it's not a generally recognised fact that kings and the most bloodthirsty of pirates share the same moral code but it's no less true for all that. It's the Power you see, it corrupts from the inside out. Any position of power brings on this condition. You can see it in your teachers at school and you will certainly find it in your bosses when you enter the job market. Behind the fancy suits and dresses lie hearts of ice and steel. And they are all quite barking mad. King George's natural tendencies were not helped on regaining consciousness to find the ship's dentist's hands in his mouth.

"Kill somebody! Kill somebody! Kill somebody!" he yelled, pushing the dentist aside and sitting bolt upright.

"Somebody touched the King! My Royal Highness has been vandalised! Head must roll!"

"I quite agree, your Supreme Monarch," said Captain Righteous. "The man will be keel hauled immediately as an example to all. Arrange the ropes, Seaman Dunnington."

Now as we learned from Hiss earlier in the story, keel hauling is a fearsome thing. Some (usually the people experiencing it first hand) would call it barbaric. It's a fairly simple operation that guarantees maximum impact on the player. A rope is stretched around and under the hull of the vessel. The player is then attached to the rope and pulled down, under, around and up back onto the deck. It doesn't sound too bad on paper but it's all in the playing as Captain Murderer soon found out. Trussed to the rope he was flung overboard while six jolly jack tars pulled on the other end of the rope, pulling him under and around the ship. Unlike Hiss, Murderer didn't mind the wet bits so much as the sharp bits as he was dragged against the splintery wooden planks of the vessel. Somehow a huge barnacle attached itself to his nose on the first trip round. By the time of his twelfth trip he looked like a piece of raw liver used as a pin cushion with a barnacle on its nose.

"Let that be a lesson to everyone not to head butt a member of the Royal Family," declared Righteous, standing with one foot on the spluttering beached Murderer.

All but two members of the crew took the lesson on board, even down to writing a note to the effect in their Church Diaries. But both Dr. Bruit and the gasping Captain Murderer made a mental note that they would one day pay back the King and all his blessed family before making a smoothie out of their brains. For as your teachers will tell you, some students are simply unteachable.

CHAPTER THE TWELFTH
WELL AND TRULY IN THE SOUP

Donald Drivelington did his best to appear delighted at the return of his daughter and the arrival of her classmates, but his best was evidently not good enough.

"Daddy, dear," said Beatrice as she danced around him in the hallway. "You look funny and sweaty and a little upset. Aren't you simply over the moon to see me again?"

"Err... no. Not really," said Drivelington. "I... I've come down with some dreaded pox that the sailors brought home from the South China Seas. The Black Formosa Corruption they call it. It's already taken off all the servants and ... err... I've had to send your mother away to keep her away from the contagion."

To Drivelington's surprise and consternation, a strange, scrawny young lad began holding his sides and rocking backwards and forwards with laughter at this. "Black Formosa Corruption? Sounds nasty. Bwa-ha-ha! Love it. We escape from a looney of a headmaster, a crazy pirate, deadly mermaids and now we all die of a tropical disease in the depths of sunny Cornwall. Priceless. You couldn't make it up."

"Stop it, Roger," said Katey. "Mr. Drivelington, you needn't worry about us. We're used to all sorts of disease at Brakem Academy. We'll be fine. In fact Billy Bones is quite a good nurse, aren't you, Billy?"

Billy nodded his head. "If you say so. I haven't really saved any lives but I'm quite good at making people comfortable in their last moments. Do you want me to examine you?"

"No," said Drivelington stepping back. "No. Look. I'm busy right now. Convalescing and things. So first thing in the morning you should go back to school."

"But Daddy," wailed Beatrice. "The headmaster wants to kill us all. Don't send us back."

"Yeah, have a heart. Let us die of the Black Formosa Corruption instead," giggled Jolly Roger.

"Okay, you can stay for the moment," said Drivelington, hoping he would have come up with a plan by morning. "But don't come any closer. I want you to stay in the East Wing and away from the West Wing, it's infected. And on no account go into the courtyard. Okay?"

"Yes, Daddy," said Beatrice. "Come on everyone. Let me show you the green room. It's really, really, really the best room ever."

"I likesss green roomssss," said Hiss, as he followed the children down the hallway and tugged his forelock at the frowning Mr. Drivelington.

"Glad to hear it," said Drivelington. "You'll love this one. Run along and enjoy."

But Hiss did not follow the children towards the green room. Instead he followed his nose, a nose trained by long years in the company of Captain Murderer, a nose that could sniff blood like a cheesemaker sniffs cheese, or a perfumier sniffs perfume or a person who loves stinky feet sniffs stinky feet. Hiss did not particularly like the scent of blood but as a rule when confronted by it he liked to discover the reason and cause of it, in order to preserve his own skin. He followed the smell down a long winding corridor until he came to a conservatory filled with lush plants, some of which he recognised as Caribbean in origin.

"Hmmm, mussst be the warmth from the glassss that makesss them grow here," he mused. He had always been fond of plants. Maybe it was the greenness that attracted him. However, he ignored the beauty of the flora and followed his nose to an open window that opened onto the centre courtyard. "Licky," he said softly, seeing the small black dog who was gobbling up a feast fit for a cannibal king. He did not know that the dead woman was Beatrice's mother, but he knew she was dead and he knew immediately that Beatrice's father had been lying about the outbreak of Black Formosa Corruption.

***

The kids spent the rest of the day in Beatrice's bedroom, playing with her doll's house and collection of stuffed animals. Even Katey and Sam who were too old for dolls and toys were entranced by this step backwards into an idyllic childhood that neither of them had ever had the opportunity to experience first hand.

After an hour or two, Katey approached Sam and took him out into a corridor. "Sam, what are we going to do?"

Sam ran his fingers through his untidy hair. "Stay here for a while?"

"We can't. Beatrice's Dad doesn't want us here. Besides there's too many of us."

"We could stay for a day or two. The others like it here. Even Jolly Roger has stopped laughing. I've never seen him so relaxed."

Katey wasn't sure. "I don't know. There's something about this place. It's too perfect. It's not for the likes of us. We were never meant to be happy, Sam."

Sam touched her cheek gently and smiled. "I'm happy now. Aren't you?"

Katey nodded. "Yes. But it won't last. I know it won't."

"Look, give us a few days to build up our strength. Then we'll move on. Yes?"

"Yes. Together?" Her eyes were hopeful.

"Of course. Always together. We're like blood and guts. We go together hand in hand." He reached for her hand, blushing. Katey blushed too as she took it. He thought about kissing her, but he didn't want to spoil things.

***

The gong gonged, summoning the inhabitants of Bollingbrook Hall to dinner. The children had just finished watching the sunset through Beatrice's favourite window.

"Oh, maybe the servants have come back," said Beatrice. "Or maybe Daddy has cooked us something special for dinner. Come on, let's find out."

She ran down the stairs, the others trailing after, stomachs rumbling at the thought of what delicious food a classy joint like Bollingbrook Hall might have to offer. They saw Mr. Drivelington coming in from his study, he had not dressed for dinner and seemed distracted and worried, which indeed he was, for he had passed the afternoon wondering how to dispose of his wife's body before his daughter or her friends discovered her. His day had been made worse just twenty minutes earlier when he had finally worked up the courage to return to the scene of the crime, only to find the body was no longer there.

"Did you make something for din-dins, Daddy?" asked Beatrice, leaping into his arms and making him stagger back against a suit of armour that had once belonged to his wife's great great great grandfather.

"No."

"Oh. Did Cook come back?"

"I don't know."

He put her down and entered the dining room. He found the large table had been set for all and a delicious smell of meat was drifting in from the kitchens.

"Christopher Columbus!" cried Sam staring around the dining hall at the cut glass chandeliers and the beautiful landscape paintings that adorned every wall. "What a place."

"Take your seatssss pleassse," said Hiss, coming in from a side room, a chef's hat perched askew on his pointy head, giving him a rakish air.

When everyone was seated he disappeared and returned a moment later carrying a large steaming pot. He was happy. Happier than he had ever been. He had prepared a real treat for his new friends. It was one of Captain Murderer's favourite dishes and Hiss had been dying for the opportunity to present it to his new masters.

"Ssssoup firssst," he said, happily, skittering nervously from seat to seat ladling the steaming broth into everyone's bowl. When he was done, he left the pot in the centre of the table and was about to go back to the kitchen when Katey stopped him.

"Hiss, won't you be eating with us?" she asked.

"No. Captainsss saysss I ssspoilsss people'sss appetitessss."

"Rubbish. Come and sit with us."

"Yes, Hiss, please do," said Beatrice, patting the empty chair beside her. "Come and sit next to me. You're my favourite pirate in the whole wide world. And I love the way you say your s's. It's the funniest sound ever."

Hiss blinked back a tear and thanked Beatrice before sitting next to her and helping himself to a bowl of broth.

"This is really very good, Mr. Hiss," said Beatrice's father, who hadn't really wanted to eat but found the broth delicious.

"Yes, bravo, Hiss. You must teach me the recipe," said Billy Bones. "I could drink this every day."

"Bessst not too," said Hiss. "Ingredientsss is hard to find."

"Can I have some more?" asked Mr. Drivelington, reaching for the pot.

"Yesss, plenty for everyone."

Mr. Drivelington reached for the ladle and screamed as he looked down into the pot.

"Daddy?" asked Beatrice becoming slightly alarmed. She stood on her chair and peered over the table and into the pot. "Mummy? What are you doing in the soup?"

This was too much for the others. In an instant everyone was on their feet and craning their necks to peer into the soup pot, where they saw a woman's head floating in soup, along with a handful of chopped carrots and onions.

Hiss realised that things were not going as planned. In his past life whenever body parts had been found in a meal it had been a cause for great hilarity not horror. "It adds to the tassssste," he said, trying to calm them. "I found it in the courtyard. It sssseeemed a shame to let it go to wassssste."

Mr. Drivelington did his best not to smile at this change in his fortunes. He stood up and pointed at his daughter. "Beatrice. I invite you into my home and find that instead of my beloved daughter, you have become a viper. A viper who would eat her mother for a starter."

"And main courssse," said Hiss. "She is roasssting nicely in the ovensss. I'm just doing the cracklingsss now."

Mr. Drivelington stifled a laugh and turned it into a sob. "Maniacs, murderers, pirates. I am afraid I must report you all to the authorities. Beatrice, it breaks my heart but there is nothing worse than a matricide. You and your friends must face the full punishment of the law."

Beatrice didn't understand what a matricide was but she did know that her Daddy was angry with her and that her mother's head was in a soup pot and that she had just eaten and enjoyed that soup. It was too much to bear. She began to sob hysterically.

Mr. Drivelington walked to the door. "I am going to fetch the justice of the peace. I expect you all to wait for my return."

"No," said Sam. He reached for the soup pot and flung it at the back of Mr. Drivelington's head. The contents of the pot slopped all over him as he fell, stunned to the floor.

"Come on," said Katey. "We're getting out of here."

"Daddy," wailed Beatrice, running to her father.

Hiss hurried to join them but Katey stopped him. "Not you. You murdered that girl's mother and then fed her to us for dinner. You're as bad as Captain Murderer."

"No. No one isss badder than him, missstressss. Hisss not murder woman. Hisss find body and cook it. Wassssste not want not."

Katey remembered Mr. Drivelington telling them all that he had sent his wife away to avoid contagion. She looked at the unconscious figure and turned to Beatrice. "Beatrice, I'm sorry but Hiss didn't hurt your mother. Your father did. He murdered her and now he wants to blame you for it."

Beatrice's eyes, were wide with shock. "No. No. Not my favourite Daddy. He couldn't."

"He could," said Sam. "He could and he has. Now come on. We have to go before he wakes up."

"I could killsss him. Make more sssoup?" said Hiss.

"No!" yelled every child in unison. "No more soup made from people. Got that?"

Hiss sighed. "Not even on sssspecial occassssionsss?"

"No. Now, come, on, let's go."

Sam picked Beatrice up and placed her over his shoulder as they headed back towards the *Jolly Bloodbath*, Licky following behind them, carrying what looked suspiciously like a bare foot in his mouth.

CHAPTER THE THIRTEENTH
THE CONTEST

Have you ever dragged your teeth down an old fashioned blackboard? Try it and you will find that the sound created raises the hackles on your body and everyone else in the room. It's a fun party trick to play when you've got your presents and are ready for the guests to leave. It clears the room in seconds. Queenie, Sea Hag ruler of the Sirens, had no blackboard. She didn't need one. Her dulcet tones would evacuate a city. Sitting on the Devil's Fangs, the place not Satan's gnashers, Queenie was practicing her scales as the Sirens frolicked in the crashing waves around her. We say scales but, in truth, it was scale in the singular. One high pitched, nerve-wrending eternal note. Even when she stopped, the note played on in your head. It hadn't always been this way. Once she had been a little girl and the Sirens her little girlfriends. They won every singing competition in their hometown in Greece. One Christmas Eve they had gone carol singing and, losing their way in a snow storm, found themselves at a palace door atop Mount Olympus.

"Perhaps the owner of this palace will give us shelter until the storm passes if we sing him a nice carol," said Queenie (her name at the time was Bambos, which means sickly sweet). "What should it be, girls?"

Well, the long and short of it is that they made a poor choice in '*Jesus, No Greater God Than Thee*'. Not a bad song by any means but possibly the worst song imaginable to sing to the owner of the palace, Zeus, father of the Greek Gods. Zeus was not a Christian, preferring to worship himself over the new boy on the block. As the carol wound its way down his front hall and into his living room he looked up from his pipe and newspaper.

"Carol singers! Again!" he snarled. This was the fifth time today and he decided that enough was enough. "Something must be done to put a stop to this nonsense at once! But what..?" The options are always enormous when you are a god, from turning people into pelicans to flooding the whole world. "Now what should it be? Hebe and Gebe, bring the cause of that racket into my presence."

"Aw, Dad! We're in the middle of a game," moaned Hebe, counter and dice in her hand.

"Maybe they'll go away if we're very quiet," suggested Gebe, Zeus's 380th son and first child from urinating upon a bull's hide (don't ask).

"How can one man have 380 completely useless children," muttered Zeus to himself, slopping down the hall in his slippers to throw open the front door, where Bambos and the girls had just reached the line "...*and all mankind shall kneel before him and spit upon false gods of old...*"

"Merry Christmas!" said Bambos, smiling up into the old god's face. "Can we please take shelter from the storm so that we may return to our town and continue our good evangelical work raising awareness of the one true God?"

Zeus glared down into the innocent smiling faces. "So you want to spread the word, do you?" he asked. "And just who do you intend spreading the word to?"

"Oh, everyone," answered Bambos. "From the little birds that sing in the trees to the little fishes of the deep ocean." And so the fate of Bambos and her girlfriends was sealed. With a wave of his hand, some magic words, and a sexy twirl from his conjuring assistant Nemea, the girls were transported in a clap of thunder and a puff of green smoke to the Devil's Fangs where they had remained ever since.

"Sing to your God from there!" Zeus yelled, slamming his front door in a theatrical manner known only to the Greek Gods.

That was so long ago. Living in the open air all the year round on a mainly fish diet had not been kind to the girls as we have already described. Fashion and make-up routines had been the first things to suffer, and their minds had been the last. Now they were as one with their appearance - Ghastly. Queenie was putting the finishing touch to a new song she was writing. The lyrics went like this:

Hate, hate...

Chorus: *Hate, hate, hate, hate, hate, hate, hate, hate, hate, hate, hate, hate, hate, hate, hate, hate...*

Repeat first verse.
Repeat Chorus.
Repeat first verse.
Repeat Chorus.
Repeat first verse to fadeout.

As she came to the end of the song, the Sirens rose as one from the choppy sea to applaud.

"Wonderful!" said Daisy.

"You really make that song your own," said Titty, wiping a tear from her eye.

"You don't just have the look, Queenie, you have the whole package!" declared Sandy.

"One million percent beautiful!" shouted Betsy.

"That was dope, dope, dope," gushed Bet-I-na.

Queenie was taking a bow when a curling piece of parchment blew up from across the ocean and hit her in the face. "What's this?" she asked, unrolling the paper. *"Have you got a talent?"* Queenie read from the scroll. *"'Britain's foremost team of talent spotters will be at the Mermaid Tavern every Monday night hoping to discover you. Your chance to win a purse of fifteen golden guineas and to appear on the Royal Variety Show in front of King George and members of the Royal Family. Don't delay, apply today!'"*

Queenie stood up on the rock with a squelch of skin and waved the scroll at the Sirens. "This is it, girls. It's taken centuries but we're back on the music scene. Fetch my guitar and hair dye."

CHAPTER THE FOURTEENTH
THE JUSTICE OF THE PEACE

Donald Drivelington awoke with a lump the size of a cannonball on the back of his head. He groaned, and tried to sink back into unconsciousness, but his wife's soup stained head was staring at him with what seemed like sullen reproach from under the table. He tried turning his back on the head but it was no good, he could feel his wife's unblinking stare burning into the back of his already aching skull. He sat up and considered his options, none of which were particularly good.

"I can hand myself in and confess," he thought to himself. "It really is the least I can do. Certainly they will hang me for murder, but the world would probably be a better place without me in it. My daughter would inherit Bollingbrook Hall and I'm sure she would put it to better use than I ever would."

This, gentle reader, I am sure you will agree, would be the option that anyone with a shred of human decency and remorse would take. However, you must take into account the fact that Donald Drivelington, while not in the same league as Dr. Bruit when it came to cruelty, or Captain Murderer when it came to joyful bloodletting, was at best a selfish man, a selfish man who had, on impulse, murdered his wife. In his defence, if he could take that mad impulsive moment back, he would, but alas, he could not. He was a murderer. Now, it is true he bore no malice towards his daughter, but if it came to a choice between him watching her hang or her watching him hang, he believed that he would be able to cope with the grief better than she would. In many ways, letting her hang for the murder of her mother would be kinder than letting her see him hang for the crime. Who knows what kind of psychological damage that would inflict upon her still developing psyche? Then he thought again. Perhaps there was no need for either of them to hang. Perhaps he could blame the crime upon her companions. Wouldn't it be better to hang that awful Hiss thing and those scruffy children rather than his own daughter? Yes, it would. It was the sensible option. He would alert the authorities and tell them that his daughter had been kidnapped by runaways who had murdered his wife. If Beatrice contradicted him, he could always have her placed in an asylum for a few years. No jury on Earth would take the word of those filthy children over the word of an English gentleman. It just wouldn't be right.

He staggered to his feet and set off towards the Mermaid Tavern, in the hopes of finding Squire Swinton, the local justice of the peace. It was now fully dark, the moon hidden behind clouds and the path along the cliffs was strewn with rocks and boulders, making this a particularly hazardous route, especially for one suffering from a not too mild form of concussion. However, Donald Drivelington's physical strength was greater than his moral fibre and after almost going bum over nose into the sea on several occasions, he eventually came in sight of the comforting lights of his destination.

***

Within the snug of the Mermaid Tavern, Squire Swinton and Bill Smithers, the landlord, were busily chopping up the remains of a family of happy campers from London, who had ventured down to Cornwall in the hopes of a nice holiday break.

"Nice bit of meat on these here bones," said Smithers, the landlord. "Our Cindy will be able to make some very tasty pasties out of 'em."

"I'm sure she will," said the good Squire, a large, jolly, red-faced man who looked as if he had enjoyed more pasties than was strictly good for him. "Here, you can take the gen'lman's cufflinks. I'll take his timepiece."

"I reckons the timepiece is worth more than the cufflinks," said the landlord, scowling with suspicion. He had been in partnership with Squire Swinton for many a year but even now he did not fully trust him.

"Aye, well, you're right there, Bill, which is why you gets two cufflinks and I only gets one timepiece. And I'll throw in his hanky too."

"Yer a scholar an' a gen'lman," said the landlord, temporarily overcome with remorse for mistrusting his business partner. "Ah, tourism ain't what it was though. Normally, we'd have five or six families a week. This is the only one we've slaughtered all month."

"Aye, well, a bit of hardship never hurt no one," said the Squire.

"Yes it did," said the landlord. "It's okay for you. You've got your livestock. Waylayin' an' killin' innocent wayfarers' just a hobby for you. Me, I've only got the locals to rely on an' we killed most of them. I can't even afford to pay the barmaid this month."

Squire Swinton shrugged. "Aye well. It's swings and roundabouts, ain't it?"

"I suppose it is," said Bill Smithers, not quite knowing what the Squire meant.

At that moment the door opened and Cindy Smithers, the landlord's wife entered the snug. "Drivelington's looking for you," she said with a nod at the squire.

"What's he want me for?" asked the Squire.

Cindy shrugged. "Dunno. Jus' passin' on the message. Didn't know I'd have to interrogate him."

Squire Swinton stared hard at Bill Smithers. "You know what he wants?"

"No. I serves drink an' I kills travellers. Mind readin' ain't one of my talents. Why don't you go ask him?"

Squire Swinton saw the wisdom in this. "Very well. Cindy, give him a tankard of your finest ale."

"We don't have a finest ale," said Cindy. "They're all horrible."

"Then give him your least horrible. Please?"

Cindy winked at him. "Very good, Squire."

***

Donald Drivelington did not accept Cindy's offer of a drink on the house, which was probably just as well, since the house ale consisted of one of the strongest poisons known to men. When Squire Swinton emerged from the snug, he was surprised to see his neighbour still alive, let alone standing on his own two feet.

"Donald, what is it I can do for you on this fine night?" he asked, signalling for a tankard of gin.

"My wife has been murdered," said Drivelington, trying not to sound too over the top.

"Ah well, worse things happen at sea," said Squire Swinton, not quite grasping the seriousness of the statement.

"Maybe they do," said Drivelington, "but even so, it is pretty hard when your home is invaded, your daughter kidnapped, your wife murdered and your fortune stolen by a gang of bandits and pirates."

"Fortune? Stolen?" Squire Swinton became more interested.

"Yes," said Donald. The bit about the fortune had been an after-thought, but an inspired afterthought. If the kids had any money or valuables on them at their time of capture then surely they would be handed over to him upon their capture.

"Then let's bring the blackguards and muckrakes to justice," said Swinton feeling more alive than he had in years. "Smithers! Summon the yeoman of the guard!"

Moments later, Bill Smithers emerged from the snug, clutching a rusty blunderbuss. "Yeoman of the guard all present, sir!" he yelled.

"Then let us go rescue this gentleman's daughter, retrieve his fortune and avenge the murder of his fair wife," said Squire Swinton, removing his pistol from his belt and charging towards the door.

"And where do you think you're going?" bawled Cindy from behind the bar, stopping the intrepid lynch mob in their tracks.

"To apprehend a gang of murderers and cutthroats," answered the Squire.

"Not tonight you're not," snapped Cindy. "It's talent night tonight. I'll have my hands full enough without you lot running off to play at soldiers."

Squire Swinton looked at Smithers and Smithers looked at Drivelington, then all three looked at their boots, afraid to meet the glare of the angry barmaid.

At length she relented a little. "Listen, you boys stay here and help out and then when I ring for last orders you can go out and apprehend whoever you like. Is that fair enough?"

Squire Swinton nodded his head and smiled sheepishly at Drivelington. "I suppose so. Your wife's already dead, ain't she? So there's no real rush. I'd hate to miss talent night. Let's stay a while, you look like you need cheering up a bit."

Drivelington didn't really want to stay but he had little choice in the matter. "Very well. But it had better be good."

"Oh I don't know as it'll be good," said Bill, "but it'll be more fun than traipsing around the clifftops in the dark, that's for sure."

"Never a truer word spoken," chuckled the squire. "I'll tell you what, let's enjoy tonight's show and we'll resume our search in the morning, if the weather's nice."

"I..." Drivelington sighed and nodded his head. He was in no real rush to apprehend the children. All he wanted to do was blame them for the murder of his wife and so far he had succeeded. There really was no need to risk life and limb tearing around the countryside in the dark. "Fine." He glanced around the empty bar and timidly asked Cindy, "Err... not being funny or anything but if tonight's talent night, shouldn't there be some talent? There's only us here and while I can play the spoons a little, I wouldn't really say it's a talent."

"Oh, don't you worry about the talent," said Bill. "The talent'll show. Give it time."

CHAPTER THE FIFTEENTH
ALL ROADS LEAD TO THE MERMAID

King George had grown tired of pirate hunting as they came in sight of the Devil's Fangs, he pointed an imperious finger towards land and ordered the crew to make all haste towards the shore.

Captain Righteous was secretly relieved. Caring for the King's person and safety was a heavy burden especially when he envisaged a deadly battle in the not too distant future between himself and the bloodthirsty crew of the Jolly Bloodbath. "Very well, Sire. We shall find a hostelry and continue the search on the morrow."

"You can continue the search without me," snapped the king. "If the Lord had meant man to travel the seas he would have given us gills."

"Very good, sire. All hands to shore."

Captain Murderer, who was having his wounds treated with salt and vinegar by the ship's surgeon, raised his head in alarm. "You means to put to shore, here?"

Captain Righteous stared down his nose at the man and sniffed. "I do. What of it?"

"You can't. 'Tis madness, so it is."

"Indeed?" said Righteous. "And why is that?"

"I knows these waters. Them there's the Devil's Fangs!" He pointed into the darkness.

"And what of them?" asked Righteous. "Tis true they have an ominous sound to them, but there is no cause for alarm."

"They be the haunt of sirens, sir. Sirens that will lure us all to our doom."

"Pshaw," scoffed Righteous. "Stuff and nonsense. Piff and poppycock. Sirens indeed. I credited you for a grown man, not a frightened little girl."

It was lucky for Righteous that Murderer was still suffering the after effects of his keel hauling, or he would have been made to pay the price for his mockery. As it was, Murderer bit his tongue and promised himself that revenge would be his in time.

HMS Cheryl sailed on past the Devil's Fangs without encountering the sirens, which led to Righteous patting Murderer on the head and laughing. "See, little girl? There's no such thing as sirens, or mermaids. And if there were, they'd find us more than a match for them."

They weighed anchor and soon the crew were all safely ashore. It was then that the moon came out from behind its curtain of cloud and Captain Murderer saw the *Jolly Bloodbath* lying at anchor next to them. "By all the shades of Hades, 'tis the *Bloodbath*!" he cried, joyfully.

"Great Scott! What good eyes you have, for a little girl," said Righteous, pushing his luck to breaking point. He called to the King. "Sire, look, our prize is here."

The King, smiled. "Of course. Divine providence led us here. Send out the jolly boats and arrest the crew at once."

Righteous ordered his men back into the jolly boats and silently they rowed out to the *Jolly Bloodbath*. Bruit and Murderer were amongst the first aboard, and were quick to report that the ship was devoid of all pirates.

"They must be out scavenging the countryside," sniffed the King. "Never mind. Mount a guard here and the rest of you shall accompany me to the nearest tavern. We shall capture our prize with the aid of the dawn's good light."

And so it was that Righteous appointed twelve good sailors to stand watch, while he, Bruit and Murderer accompanied the King inland towards the Mermaid Tavern, whose lights could be seen twinkling from the clifftop above them.

The King wasn't overjoyed by the Captain's choice of travelling companions and he voiced his displeasure, loud and long as they trailed up the footpath away from the cove. "Why would you choose those two to escort us? Both are ugly as sin and one of them has insulted one, freely and loudly. He should be in chains, not gallivanting around the countryside with us."

"Your grace is right as ever," answered Righteous, "however, these roads are infested with footpads, cutpurses and all manner of villains. I thought perhaps the frightening faces of these two sturdy gentlemen would deter any thieves or criminals from attempting to do us harm."

Murderer felt the rage begin to burn in his belly, until his brother placed a hand on his shoulder to calm him down. "Shh. He means no harm. In many ways he be flattering us. We do have frightening faces do we not?"

Murderer nodded his head in agreement. "Aye. I suppose we do. I'll let it slide this time."

***

Katey, Sam, Hiss and the rest of their not so merry band of outlaws had made their way from Bollingbrook Hall towards the *Jolly Bloodbath*, with great haste. Beatrice, was crying hysterically and didn't notice that they had taken the wrong path which instead of returning them to the ship, took them out onto Cradlesnip Moor, an inhospitable place, with nothing but a ruined church and a disused pickling factory to recommend it.

They stopped for a while to rest in the churchyard. Hiss, who had grown fond of Beatrice, was desperate to make amends for cooking her mother's head in the soup. He tried to cheer her up by dancing a little jig around the ancient gravestones.

"Pleasssse, Beatrice," he pleaded. "Hisssss issss ssssorry, Hissss not know it wassss Beatrice'ssss Mummy'sss head."

Licky trotted over and licked the disconsolate Hiss on the nose. This made Beatrice smile. "Licky likes you."

"Yessss, Licky likesss Hisss becaussse Hisss gives him a nice meal of liver and kidneysss for din-dinsss," said Hiss, patting the little dog. "They issss nice kidneyssss, yessss, Licky?" Licky licked him again in confirmation, but Beatrice was crying again, possibly because she had just realised who those nice liver and kidneys had belonged to.

Sam had finally managed to light a fire in the doorway to the ruined church. Its heat was meagre but his classmates gathered around it like moths, holding out their hands to receive what little comfort it had to offer.

"Good work, Sam," said Katey.

Sam felt himself blushing at her words. "What do we do now?"

Katey shrugged. "I don't know. We should get back to the ship. Beatrice's Dad won't be happy with us when he wakes up."

"Here, what's this?" said Billy Bones, noticing a faded poster that hung upon the door to the church.

Reading, writing and arithmetic had never been rated highly in the curriculum at Brakem Hall Academy, however, Beatrice could read perfectly. She was still weeping away, in mourning for her mother, but Sam called to her anyway. "Beatrice, could you help us?"

The little girl looked up and sniffed. "What is it?"

"Can you read something for us?"

A faint look of hope crossed her tear-stained face for an instant. "Is it a fairy story? Is it a romance? Is it a kissing story?"

"I know not," said Sam. "Perhaps you could tell us."

Beatrice trotted forward. "You'll have to get out of the light. It's too dark to see."

The children stepped back, allowing the flames from the fire to cast their flickering light upon the poster.

"*'Have you got a talent? Britain's foremost team of talent spotters will be at the Mermaid Tavern every Monday night hoping to discover you. Your chance to win a purse of fifteen golden guineas and to appear on the Royal Variety Show in front of King George and members of the Royal Family. Don't delay, apply today!'*" Beatrice finished reading and turned to her friends, her face alive with excitement. "Oh, goody! A talent show. Can we enter? It will be such fun and we will get to meet the King. I love kings. They wear lovely clothes."

"I... but..." Sam was unsure. "Beatrice, we don't have any talent."

"Yesss we do, Sssam," hissed Hiss. "Hisss can dance."

76

"And Licky can wag his tail and walk on his back legs," said Beatrice. "I bet the King will love seeing Hiss and Licky dance."

"He could see us all dance," said Katey. "We could be a dancing troupe. Go on, Sam, it'll be fun."

"But I can't dance," said Sam.

"Neither can any of us," giggled Jolly Roger. "It'll be hilarious."

Beatrice began tugging at his sleeve. "Oh go on. Do say yes. You could even sing a love song with Katey."

"I..." he felt himself burning up with shame. "A love song? With Katey? D-don't be ridiculous."

"I don't think it would be ridiculous," said Katey. "I think it would be fun."

"But..."

Katey felt embarrassed too now. "Of course, it's just a show. It doesn't mean we really love each other."

"Err... no. Course it doesn't. I... well, yeah. Okay. Come on, let's find this Mermaid Tavern then. It beats sitting around out here all night."

CHAPTER THE SIXTEENTH
CURTAIN UP

"Open up! In the name of the King!" Captain Righteous bellowed as he banged upon the tavern door with his gloved fists.

Nobody came to the door. From within the travellers could hear the sound of fiddles and flutes and raucous laughter.

Righteous hammered upon the door again. "Open up, I say!"

With a sigh, Dr. Bruit stepped forward. "If I may?" He pushed open the door. "Ain't no need for knockin'. This is a public house. All are welcome. Even the likes of us."

They entered the tavern and found it filled with locals. A trio of musicians were playing badly upon a small stage whilst three men sat in high backed chairs, watching with interest. The rest of the inhabitants were busy drinking, jesting and playing dice. The room fell silent as they entered and the three men in the high-backed chairs turned to stare at the newcomers.

"If you're here for the talent show, sign your names at the bar and wait your turn," said the man in the centre chair.

"Talent show?" snorted Captain Righteous. "We are here on the King's business. Bow down before your liege."

The man in the centre chair stood and stared and then took a coin from his purse and looked at it. His face went pale as he recognised the face on the back of the coin. "Sire!" he cried, going down on his knees. "Squire Swinton at your service."

The King nodded his head, impatiently. "Get back on your feet, man."

Swinton stood and bowed. "You are too kind, sire. May I present your servants, Donald Drivelington and Bill Smithers, the landlord of this fine establishment. We are at present judging a talent contest in your name. The winners shall perform for your Grace at the Royal Variety Show next year."

The King shuddered. "A pox upon the variety show and all who perform in it."

Swinton frowned. "Do I take it my King does not enjoy the Variety show?"

"You may," snapped the King. "I detest it."

"Then you are in luck, sire. For tonight you may judge the contestants yourself and see which you would like to see perform again at the show. For once, you will have a Royal Variety Show that you really want to see."

The King saw little sense in this. "All that means is that I get to see the same foul acts twice instead of once. Bring me your finest wine and a plate of plover's eggs."

"Of course, but while you eat, perhaps you would do us the honour of judging the contestants yourself?"

The King sighed. "Very well, but if any act displease me I shall have them flogged."

"Commendable!" cried the Squire. "Perhaps your companions would like to sit with you and be your fellow judges?"

"It would be an honour," said Righteous, bowing.

Murderer and Bruit looked at each other and shrugged their monstrous shoulders. "Aye, why not? There be little else to do."

***

Over the course of the next forty five minutes, the King had ordered three jugglers to be flogged, a boy band called Lucky Lutes to be hung by their tongues from the ceiling and four magicians and their assistants to be burned alive for practicing witchcraft. Captain Murderer found himself warming to the King.

"You know, maybe I was too hard on him," he confided to Bruit as they applied thumbscrews to a comedian who had failed to make the King laugh. "The lad certainly knows how to have a good time."

"Aye," agreed Bruit. "He does that."

"Tighter, break his thumbs," ordered the King, who was now beside himself with mirth. "Let's show him the penalty for failing to amuse his King."

"AAAAARRRGH!" wailed the comedian. "I'm soooorrry."

"Who's next?" asked Righteous. "Come on, don't keep your King waiting."

Surprisingly, many of the young hopefuls who had turned up at the Mermaid Tavern that evening, hoping to take a short cut to fame and fortune had become disillusioned with the idea.

"AAAARGHHHH!" wailed the poor comedian as Murderer gave an extra twist of the thumbscrew.

It was then that Sam, Katey and the others entered the tavern. "We're here for the talent show," said Sam. "We're the... er... we're the..."

"The Dancing Buccaneers," said Katey, proudly and we're here to dance for the King."

"Go on then, get up on the stage and show 'em what you can do," said Bill Smithers, the barman.

The group pushed there way through the crowd to the stage and took their bows.

"And you are?" said the King, staring down his nose at them.

"We are the Dancing Buccaneers, Sire," said Sam.

"Indeed?" answered the King. "An apt name. We like to watch buccaneers dance, don't we, Righteous?"

"We do?" asked Righteous, who was a little slow when it came to picking up on the King's rather ponderous wit..

"Yes, indeed. We like to watch them dance on the end of a rope."

The audience roared with laughter. All except, Bruit, Murderer and Donald Drivelington.

"Them's my kids," cried Bruit. "They robbed me an' ran away from my care."

"That's my Hiss!" roared Murderer pointing at a bewildered looking Hiss who was doing his best to hide behind Beatrice. "I raised him from a mere slip of a thing to what he is today, an he repays me by stealin' my ship an' falling in with these cutthroats."

"And that's my daughter and those are the villains who murdered my darling wife," cried Donald Drivelington.

"Massssterrrr?" said Hiss, staring into the crowd. "Issss that my lovely Captainssss?" He bounded from the stage and leaped into Murderer's arms, showering him in wet, slimy kisses.

"Gerroff me, foulness!" roared Murderer, hurling him back towards the stage so that he landed on top of poor little Beatrice.

The King stood and called for quiet. He looked at Murderer and Bruit and Drivelington. "Are these accusations true?"

"Which ones?" asked Murderer, before his brother nudged him in the ribs. "Oh, yes, Sire, they's true. They be the pirates who stole the *Jolly Bloodbath* and sank your ship."

"Then today really is my lucky day," smiled the King. "Clap them in irons."

Drivelington attempted to speak with the King on his daughter's behalf. "Excuse me, Sire, but the little girl is innocent. The others murdered my wife, but she had no hand in it. I swear."

The King shrugged. "She was with the others when they sank our ship and drenched our person. Therefore she is guilty of piracy. And you, sir, have failed as a parent. I always say it is the parents who are to blame for the crimes of our children. You sir, have been lax in your duty. You are as guilty as she is."

"No, sire," cried Drivelington. "She... she's not even really mine. I... I won her in a raffle one Christmas and gave her as a present to my wife. But she was always a wild one. I tried my best to tame her, sire."

"But you failed," sighed the King. "Very well, we shall be merciful and spare your life, but I expect you to come and bear witness when we hang the child at Traitor's Dock."

"Err... yes, of course, sire," Drivelington dropped to his knees weeping with gratitude. "With pleasure, your highness."

Now, this being a tale of pirates and piracy, you are no doubt thinking it is high time we had some good old fashioned swash buckling action, the clash of tempered steel on steel, nimble swordplay on a stone stairwell. Well, read on, we can't supply the stairwell, but perhaps some errant swordplay could be called forth.

Sam, seeing Righteous, Murderer and Bruit moving forwards to apprehend them, turned wildly, looking for the nearest exit. Alas, the nearest exit would mean hurdling over his enemies, so instead, he looked for weapons, seeing a pair of handsome rapiers hanging upon the wall, he ran for them, and slashed the air in front of him.

"Keep back, or you'll be sorry," he swore.

Righteous drew his sword and smiled, sadly. "Boy, I would not slay you. Put up your arms and come quietly."

Sam spat on the sawdust at his feet. "You wouldn't slay me, but you would drag me back to London and watch me die on the end of a rope. No thank you, sir. I prefer to die with steel in my hand."

He sprang forward and lunged, but Righteous parried the blow with ease. You may well expect our hero to be an expert with a sword, but this was not the case. Sam had never had the opportunity to learn the noble art of fencing, whereas Righteous had been trained in the arts of war since his first day in the nursery.

Righteous was pressing Sam back towards the wall. He felt helpless and weak. He tossed a flagon of ale at the captain, but apart from staining his tunic it caused him no harm.

While Righteous attempted to subdue Sam, Murderer and Bruit were rounding up the others. "Come here, you little whelp," growled Murderer, snatching Beatrice up from the floor and shaking her like a baby's rattle. "You've got a whole world of suffering coming your way before they hangs you."

Hiss watched this from his hiding place under a table. He was feeling severely conflicted. Torn between his old life and his new one. Here was his beloved Captain Murderer, throttling the lovely Beatrice who had only treated Hiss with kindness, even after he had cooked her own mother for dinner. Licky, the dog was snapping at Murderer's heels, until a well aimed kick, from a sturdy boot, sent him sliding across the floor to join Hiss under the table. Hiss patted the dog. "Shhh. It'ssss okay, Licky. It'ssss okay." He looked at Beatrice. Her face was turning blue. It looked as if Captain Murderer was trying to pull her head from her shoulders. Enough was enough. Captain Murderer had gone too far this time.

Now, it may be true that Sam had no experience of swordsplay, but Hiss on the other hand had grown up watching the best in the world. He had even practiced their moves, every night, challenging his shadow to duel to the death. Now was the time to put that training into practice. Now was the time for the scholar to prove that he was indeed a master. He scuttled out from under the table and called to Sam.

"Sssam. The other ssssword. Give Hisss the other sssword please?"

Sam pushed away from Righteous and tossed his second blade through the air. Hiss caught it nimbly and then charged towards Captain Murderer.

"Let Beatrice go!" he howled, stabbing the pirate in his enormous behind.

"Graaahhh!" Murderer howled and dropped the child. Then he turned to face his assailant, a look of pain, embarrassment and then angry surprise upon his face. "You? You dare? You miserable piece of flotsam. I'll rip your foul skin from your back and use it for a hanky." He drew his own sword and slashed the air above Hiss's head.

"Ssssorry Captainsss, but she'ssss my friend."

"You have no friends. You're a monstrous imp who should've been drowned at birth." Murderer slashed the air again, but he was too slow. Hiss ducked under his arm and jabbed the pirate in the knee with his blade. "Arrrrghhh!"

Hiss moved forward again, his face wet with tears. He knew he would have to kill his former master, but he still felt bad about it. He jabbed again, catching Murderer in the thigh, and then raised the point of his blade towards the pirate's black heart. "Goodbye, Captainssss."

THUNK!

Dr. Bruit's ham-sized fist came down upon Hiss's pointy head, knocking him senseless to the ground. Indeed, if Hiss had been a normal man, the force of the blow would have left him permanently brain damaged, but thankfully, Hiss's brain had already been damaged beyond repair and so he was merely rendered temporarily unconscious.

"Hiss! No!" wailed Beatrice, running to his side and showering him with kisses. "You horrid, horrid men. How could you?"

"Ha! That's nothing, compared to what we's gonna do to you, girly," promised Bruit. He took out a dirty dagger and pressed it to the little girl's throat. "Listen up, you lot! Throw down your weapons and surrender, or the pretty icky baby gets her gizzard slit."

Sam stared at Bruit and the helpless Beatrice, then he glanced at Righteous and knew the game was over. He dropped his sword. "Very well. I surrender."

Righteous put a hand on the boy's shoulder. "You fought bravely. Inexpertly, but bravely." Then he turned to Bruit. "Bruit, you are no gentleman."

"Never said I was, sir," smiled the monstrous headmaster, his dagger still at the young girl's throat. "But I got 'em to surrender, didn't I?"

"Indeed you did, yes, we are victorious, but what is victory without honour?" said Righteous.

Bruit thought for a moment. "Err... victory? It's still victory, ain't it?"

"Well said, sir," said the King. "When we get to London, remind me to confer a knighthood upon you, sir. Yes, victory is victory and that is all that matters. Now clap these wretches in irons. I want to go home."

It was then that Queenie and her Sirens arrived on the scene. Now, you may well be wondering how it is that they took so long to reach the Mermaid Tavern, when they had a good head start on all the others. We ask you to remember that while Sirens are possessed of arms and teeth and a strong smell, they are not, alas possessed of legs, having to make do with a large fishy tail and fins. While tails and fins are great for swimming, they are more of a hindrance when it comes to scaling cliffs and trekking across country in the dark. Where you and I are free to break into a trot or even a sprint if we feel like making haste, Queenie and her friends had no other option but to slither and slide their way across two and a half miles of rocky terrain. By the time they arrived at the Mermaid Tavern they were tired, bruised, thirsty and very, very smelly.

"Pooh! What's that stink?" cried the King, sniffing the air and gagging.

"It's probably me," said Murderer, sniffing himself, proudly.

"It's worse than you, matey, it's them," said Bill Smithers, pointing towards the Sea Hags as they ordered bottles of grog from the bar. "Oi! I told you before, you're barred, now get out."

Queenie slammed a fishy fist upon the bar. "No. We are here to win the talent show. So shutup and listen to us."

Captain Righteous stepped forward and addressed the creatures. "Madam, you are indeed a strange and wondrous being, and yet I am afraid you are too late. We have just apprehended a gang of violent and dangerous criminals and his Royal Highness has to leave immediately."

Queenie stared around the room and recognised Hiss, who was sitting on the floor, rubbing his head. "You. I remember you."

Hiss smiled at her, his heart fluttering. "Beautiful, sssinger. Hiss remembersss you too. Hasss you come to sssave usss? Isss thisss a beautiful dream? Hassss Hissss died and gone to heaven?"

"No," said Queenie. "We've come to eat you." She turned back to Righteous. "We saw them first. That's our dinner you are manhandling. Release them into our custody at once and we'll let you go just as soon as we've sung for the King."

The King had waited long enough. He pushed through the crowd and stood nose to nose with Queenie. "Enough. Out of our way or we shall have you imprisoned too."

"You are free to go, after we sing," said Queenie. "Ready, girls?"

"Girl power!" cried the Sirens before bursting into one of their favourite songs. *"Blood and guts, blood and guts, that's what makes the world go round..."*

"Enough!" cried the King. "That is quite possibly the worst singing act I've ever heard. Don't you agree, Righteous?"

Righteous nodded his head. "Yes, Sire. The one on the left has something but the others are just holding her back. It's a no from me."

"They're all rubbish," growled Murderer. "Rubbish and ugly."

This last was too much for Queenie. "Rubbish? Ugly? You... you don't know what you're talking about. Let's give them the hate song, girls."

"Hate, hate, hate...."

The girls sang at the top of their hideous voices, reaching a pitch too high for mortal men to comprehend. The ceiling cracked above them and the ground opened up beneath them as every human being present sought refuge from the hellish din in unconsciousness. Within seconds, the Mermaid Tavern, which had stood on that spot for two hundred and forty three years was no more than a pile of rubble.

Queenie looked around the ruins and saw the unconscious children, half buried under rubble.

"Shall we eat them here, Queenie, love?" asked Betsy.

Queenie shook her head. "No, babes. I've lost my appetite. Come on, let's go home. These people wouldn't know talent if it crept up behind them and bit their heads off."

"Well, we could do that," said Daisy. "Just for a laugh, like."

"No, they taste horrible out of water. Too dry. Come on girls. Home time. This smoky atmosphere's playing havoc with my skin."

And off they slithered, singing *"to the sea, to the sea, to the beautiful sea,"* all the way home.

CHAPTER THE SEVENTEENTH
LACKING ALL HOME COMFORTS

Okay, reader, here's the educational part of our story:

The human body is remarkably resilient. It can cope and shrug off allsorts of ghastly microbe diseases from smallpox to scurvy and whooping cough and even the dreaded Claxon's Bends. Break a leg and, doctored properly, if will be right as rain in a few weeks. However, if you have six tons of stone-masonry, several solid oak beams and a variety of roofing tiles dropped from a great height onto your head your chances of survival are zero unless you are an amoeba. Sadly not one of our party of pirates, soldiers, royalty, children, cannibals, monster or parent was an amoeba (other than in the sense of dress code and polite manners). Luckily for our story only one member of the party was unlucky enough to get the full load of stone-masonry, oak beams and tiles dropped directly onto their bonce. As if that wasn't enough, when the floor gave way he also got wooden splinters in his bare feet and hands as he tumbled into the cellars below. There's no easy way to tell you this but he didn't survive, which is probably a good thing as the only life he could have led after such a pummelling would have been as The Flat Boy in a travelling freak show. You might want to sit down as we tell you the name of this poor dead boy. It was Zeb Cowsill. Yes, the very same Zeb Cowsill who hasn't been named so far in our story but has been there all the same from the start. It's a little late and a bit pointless to fill you in on his background now as he's hardly likely to have much bearing on the story from hereon, but we'll just say that he was originally from St Helen's and his mother smoked a pipe. May he rest in peace (unlikely under that lot). We'll not forget him.

Amazingly, considering the devastation, whatisname was the only fatality. Oh, there were many boo-boos and hurties, and had a mother been there she would have spent a fortnight kissing scrapes and abrasions better, but, thank goodness for the sake of our tale, the only mother in the neighbourhood had been thrown from a third storey window and cooked in a soup. Several fingers, toes, eyes and ears were lost in the general melee but all our main characters survived. True they moaned a bit for a good ten minutes but, not being in the namby-pamby time period we now live in, they then picked themselves up and got on with business. Or at least they would have had each and every one of them not been weighted down by crossbeams or rubble.

"A fine to-do," declared the King, wedged tightly under one of the beams. "How on earth did my leg get in that strange position, looped over that broken table?" He managed to pick up a brick and bang it against the twisted leg.

"Ow!" shouted Captain Righteous. "That's not your leg, sire. It's mine. It was the one part of me that wasn't hurt...until now."

"A golden guinea and their own apartment in Plague Pit Lane to the first man or child who releases me from this blithering beam," said the King. Everyone struggled to pick themselves up all the harder with this incentive but after five minutes of exertion and profanity (luckily it was after the watershed) they all came to the same conclusion.

"We can't move," said Sam. "We're all stuck like flies on flypaper."

"Hopefully the local council will notice the building has come down and send out the emergency services," said Captain Righteous.

"I doubt that," said Swinton. "Me and Smithers are the local council."

"We're also the local emergency services," agreed Smithers.

"Somebody must be able to get out," said Katey. More struggling ensued.

"No...no we can't," said everyone.

"So what are we going to do, just wait here, hoping someone comes along?" asked Katey.

"Yes," said everyone, fed up and too tired to struggle any more.

"Let's sing a song to help pass the time," suggested Beatrice. "What about 'Three Cheers for Rainbows'? It goes like this: *Three cheers for rainbows, not one, not two but three cheers for rainbows. They lift your heart when rain doth fall, they greet your eyes in skies so tall, seven colours hath they from God's painting box* - OW!"

It was hard to see just who had flung the brick that knocked poor Beatrice unconscious but it was decided that there would be no more singing that night. And what an uncomfortable night it was for all concerned (and some were more concerned than others). Unless you yourself live in a semi-demolished house you can have no idea of just how irritating draughts can be, especially if you are lying on a bed of rocks and the draughts are accompanied with squally showers which at recurring intervals turn to sleet. Irritating is the word and you may be aware that many of our cast were irritable to begin with. But this night was so dreadfully upsetting to the nervous system that even little Beatrice, who spent most of it in blissful senselessness, was cursing like a demon by breakfast time.

"Oh gosh and golly!" she swore, shivering as the sleet turned to ice all over her face and arms.

"Stop moaning like a little girl!" thundered Captain Murderer who had put up with her whining for a good ten seconds.

"She is a little girl, you foul beast!" snapped Katey. Captain Murderer shook his head at such rudeness.

"What do you teach 'em at that school of yours, Bruit?" he asked. "It certainly baint manners to your elders and betters. Can't you reach over and bite her head off?"

"What do you think I've been trying to do all night?" snapped back his brother.

"Okay, you two, keep your hair on." warned Captain Righteous. "We're all in this together and the only way we'll get out of it is if we all act as a well-oiled machine."

"I'd like to well oil 'im!' muttered Bruit to some tittering from the sailors and children.

"King's navy here!" warned Righteous. "Cut out the giggling and listen hard. By my calculations there are six of us trapped by the beam holding me down. If we act as one and try to hurl it to the right on the count of three instead of all pushing and pulling in different directions we might just budge the thing." It was a good plan but one doomed to failure as three of the jolly Jack Tars under that particular beam hadn't been taught the difference between right and left in their formative years. Now well into their twenties they would have felt foolish to bring this point up

93

in front of the children who were present. So, as it turned out, on the count of three, three of Righteous's men pulled one way while the other three pulled in the opposite direction. A consequence of this was more exhaustion and more irritability.

"Neptune's teeth!" declared the King. "What kind of men do they let into my navy these days?!" Another brick flew out of the darkness to silence him. And so the day passed. And the next, which was followed by the next and then the next, by which time spirits were at an all time low down in the ruined tavern. The sun could be seen directly above for an hour each day but it's warming rays didn't reach our miserable band.

"By my calculations it must be the 7th of March," said Captain Righteous. And he was right. The 7th of March, 1755. Now those members of the Royal Family amongst our readers will be aware of the significance of that date, but, thanks to the Official Secrets Act, everyone else will be in the dark. Well, prepare to be enlightened. The 7th of March, 1755, was the date of The Second Spanish Armada. Yes, the Spanish Armada that reached our shores just south of the Devil's Fangs. After that brief explanation, let us resume our story.

"SHH!" hissed Sam. "Listen! Can you hear it?" Everyone listened but not a sound was heard until...

"There it is again!" cried Sam. "It's voices! Can you hear voices?!" He was right! There were voices and they were getting nearer to the collapsed tavern. As one everyone started to yell as loud as their fatigued bodies would allow.

"Help! Down here! Save us! Help! Please!"

There was silence for a moment and then the sound of scurrying feet. And then glory be, faces could be seen looking down at them. And then one of the faces called down to them...in Spanish.

CHAPTER THE EIGHTEENTH
THE BIG QUESTIONER

"*¿Que pasa, muchachos?*" called a man with a forked beard and a shiny steel helmet, his sharp eyes, puzzled and ever so slightly amused.

"What's he say?" asked the King.

"I'm not sure," said Righteous.

"You told me you spoke French like a native," snapped the King.

"*Oui, oui,* your Majesty, and if he were speaking to us in French I would be able to translate with ease. However..."

"*¿Hombres, necesitas ayuda, o que?*" said the man, the amusement having faded from his eyes.

"Oi! Stop talkin' gibberish an' get us out of here!" yelled Captain Murderer, who believed that curses and a booming voice worked in any language. He wasn't wrong, either. Within minutes, the steel-helmeted gent had been joined by ten more equally well-dressed bravos, who proceeded to heave and pull at the masonry and bricks and timber until at last, all the survivors of the Mermaid Tavern were free.

The King, taking his cue from Captain Murderer, bellowed his thanks to the Spanish gentlemen and then turned his attentions to Katey, Sam, Beatrice and the others. "Right, well, you've had your fun. Now it's time to pay the piper as it were. You will be accompanying us to London and your imminent execution." He turned to Righteous. "Clap them in irons."

Righteous frowned. "I'm afraid it's not quite so simple as that, Sire. Our irons are still under the rubble somewhere. Perhaps if we asked them to promise not to run away we could leave them unbound?"

"Or we could kill 'em here, an' have done with it?" suggested Murderer, hopefully.

"Very well," sighed the King. "I suppose it will save us the excuse of a trial."

Murderer reached for his pistol but found it in the hand of one of his steel-helmeted rescuers. "Hey, give that back." He looked around and saw that all the King's men had been similarly disarmed. "What's goin' on?" he asked. "Is this some kind of continental joke? Coz if it is, it's not going to go down well over here. An Englishman's pistol is his..."

"¡*Basta*!" yelled one of the steel-helmeted men.

"I beg your pardon?" snorted Murderer.

The man explained himself fully, in Spanish, which left everyone puzzled and confused until they were herded out of the ruins of the inn at sword point towards a figure in a black pointed hood and robes, perched on a white horse.

"I bring you greetings from Spain," said the man in the hood, his voice muffled by the thick cloth that covered his face.

"Eh?" said the King. "Speak up man, and don't mumble."

"I said, I bring you greetings from Spain. I am El Gran Inquisitor."

"El Gran Inquisitor?" asked the King. "You don't look like a Gran to me." He turned to Righteous. "Does he look like a Gran to you?"

"No, Sire. He looks like a chap. A chap in a hood."

"And a dress," said Bruit. "He is wearing a dress."

"Thees eees not a dress!" screamed the man in the hood. "Thees eees a holy robes."

"Well, if they're holy, I could get the Missus to fix 'em for you," said Smithers. "It's the least we can do, after you helping us out of that fix."

"¡*Silencio!*" boomed El Gran Inquisitor. "I am El Gran Inquisitor. In your barbarous tongue, it means something like... er... the big questioner. And I have a beeg question for you. Which way is it to London? For we have come to conquer all before us and to make a present of this pitiful country to His Majesty the King of Spain."

"Eh? What rot," snapped the King. "I'm King here. You do know what this means? It means war."

El Gran Inquisitor laughed a loud, evil laugh. "A war you have lost. So you are King George, eh? I should have known. They told me you were ugly. A King should be handsome."

"This coming from a fellow in a dress and a pointy hood," snorted the King. "I never heard such nonsense."

El Gran Inquisitor yelled something in Spanish and two men came forward and grabbed hold of the King, forcing him to the ground. "That ees better. You kneel like a dog before El Gran Inquisitor. You are my prisoner. You are all my prisoners. We shall sail to London in style where you will be executed in the Tower of London."

Guards manhandled them all the way back to the bay where the Spanish fleet awaited them. Along with the

Jolly Bloodbath which had been commandeered by El Gran Inquisitor's men and now flew the flag of Spain.

As they rowed towards the *Bloodbath*, Sam whispered to his friends. "We've got to do something. We can't let them execute the King."

Jolly Roger burst out laughing. "At least we'll be going out in good company."

"The King wants to execute us too, remember," said Katey.

"Everybody wants to kill us," laughed Roger. "My Mum was right, she always said I had a face you could kill for."

"Listen, if we save the King, he's sure to pardon us," said Sam.

"I wouldn't be so sure," said Katey. "I don't trust Kings. Too full of 'emselves."

"Well, I'm going to save him, with or without you," said Sam.

***

Once aboard the *Jolly Bloodbath*, the kids were forced down into the hold and locked in tight. El Gran Inquisitor decided to put off sailing until the morning. In the meantime, he lived up to his name as he set about questioning his prisoners, one by one, throughout the night. He began with the King, but soon became enraged, when the King refused to answer any questions without asking four in return.

"It is I who am the Big Questioner, not you," snapped El Gran Inquisitor.

"Sez you," sniffed the King. "I'm the King. I get to ask as many questions as I like. Why do you wear that ridiculous hood? Why have you invaded my realm? How do you hope to get away with this?"

"I... I wear this hood to fill you with fear."

"Doesn't work. It makes you look stupid."

"I have invaded your realm in revenge for your nation's acts of piracy against Spain."

"Lies and slander. Piracy is illegal throughout the realm. In fact we had just captured some notorious pirates when you came along and ruined everything."

"Pfa! You lie like a dog. We shall get away with this because I have at my command the entire Spanish Armada. The Invincible Armada that shall have you English trembling in your beds."

"Rot. Your Armada stinks and so do you."

"Enough!" El Gran Inquisitor had the King dragged away and decided to question Captain Righteous next. "You call yourself a Captain of the Royal Navy. What were you and the King doing when we captured you?"

"My name is Algernon Righteous."

"Yes, but what were you doing?"

"I am a Captain in His Majesty's Navy."

"I know these already. What were you doing here?"

"My serial number is... oh, dash it all, I can't remember my serial number. My name is Algernon Righteous."

El Gran Inquisitor had Captain Righteous dragged away and decided to question Hiss next. "What manner of creature are you?" he asked as Hiss trembled and quivered on the floor of the cabin.

"A loathsssssome creature, *sssseñor*," said Hiss.

"Are you a rare breed of monkey?"

Hiss shrugged. "Hiss doesssn't think ssso. Hiss's Mum wasssn't a monkey."

"And your father?"

"Hiss'ss Mum sssayss he wasss a drunken devil, ssseñor."

El Gran Inquisitor jumped up and clapped his hands in delight. "Priceless! Then you admit you are a devil?"

"No, Hiss say hisss Dad wasss a drunken devil."

"Then you too are a devil. And this proves that the King of England consorts with devils. Would you not agree?"

Hiss thought for a moment and pulled a lump of wax out of his ear. "Not really, Gran Inquissssitor. No. He never conssssorted with me. He did throw a brick at me once."

"Well, who did you consort with, creature?" asked El Gran Inquisitor, preparing his instruments of torture in case Hiss proved reluctant to answer his questions.

"Hisss not really sssure your Gran Inquisssitivenesss."

El Gran Inquisitor smiled beneath his hood. He sensed the moment for torture had arrived. He removed a tong from the coal brazier he had set up in the middle of the cabin. It glowed red in the gloom. "And what is it exactly that Hiss is not sure of?" he asked. "I warn you, I am not a patient man."

"Hissss not really sssure what conssssort meansss, your Inquissitivenessss, sssir."

"Ignorant beast. Is it down to me, a foreigner, to educate you in your own tongue?"

Hiss cringed before the red-hot tong, El Gran Inquisitor waved in front of him. "Only if hisss Gran Inquisssitivenessss wantssss to. Hissss doesssn't really care."

"It means to have truck with."

"Eh?" Hiss was non-plussed.

"To do business with."

Hiss felt relief wash over him. "Ah, Hiss understsstand now. Hisss not do busssinesss with anyone. Hisss not a busssinessss type of man."

"You're not a man at all, creature. You are a demon."

Hiss didn't really know what to say to that, so he said nothing.

"To consort with means to have truck with, to do business with, to have relations with..."

"Ah... Hiss have relationsss with hisss Mum and hisss Auntie Flo and hisss cousssin Eric and hisss Uncle Frank, but Hisss hasssn't sssseen them in yearssss."

"Imbecile!" roared El Gran Inquisitor. He would have branded Hiss with the red hot tongs then and there but they had cooled off and he had to return them to the coals to re-heat them. "To consort with also means to speak with..."

"Hisss ssspeak with you, your Ssspanisssshnessss."

"Not me. Who else did you speak with? Who are your friends?"

"Hiss not really have friendssss sso to sssspeak. Hisss liked his Captainsss but not any more. Hisss likessss Missssstresss Katey and he likessss Masssster Sssssam and he really likesss little Beatrice. She'ssss kind, but she'sss not happy with Hisss because Hissss cooked her Mummy'ss head in a tasssty sssoup. And Hissss likessss Licky too."

"Enough," snapped El Gran Inquisitor. "It is time for your consorts to face my questions." He ordered his men to take Hiss to a separate cabin, in which he was confined to a small cage. When his men returned, El Gran Inquisitor had Katey, Sam and Beatrice dragged before him.

"Can we have dinner, please?" asked Beatrice, who like everyone else, except Hiss, hadn't eaten all day. "I'm starving."

El Gran Inquisitor loomed over her. "It is food for the soul, you should be thinking of," he said softly, raising his hood so he could munch on a chicken drumstick.

"My soul? Are we going to pray?" Beatrice asked. "Can we sing some hymns too. I like hymns. Sometimes I write my own. Would you like to hear one?" Before El Gran Inquisitor could answer either yay or nay, she burst into the following song, *"God made the froggies, the birdies and the doggies, God made the lilies, the daisies and the rose, God made my tootsies, my fingers and my toes. Oh isn't he a clever God? Isn't he a clever God? Isn't he a clever God? He's cleverer than me and he's cleverer than you, he's cleverer than Billy and he's cleverer than Sue."* She beamed at El Gran Inquisitor. "There. Do you want to join in? I don't really know if he is cleverer than Sue, I just made her up because it rhymes with you. But it's a nice song, isn't it? Can we eat now?"

"No!" roared El Gran Inquisitor, who didn't really like singing, or little girls. "I want to know who you saw with the devil."

"I didn't see anyone with the devil. Is the devil here?" Beatrice looked scared.

"You're scaring her, you beast," said Katey, angrily. "Stop scaring her."

"She should be scared," said EL Gran Inquisitor. "You should all be scared. I have it from the devil's own lips that he has consorted with all three of you."

"Do you mean Hiss?" asked Sam. "He's not the devil. He's just an ugly little guy. That's all. He used to be a pirate but he's changed. He's not a bad lad when you get to know him."

"Not a bad lad?" said El Gran Inquisitor. In all his days in the job, nobody had ever described the devil as 'not a bad lad'. This led him to believe that he was dealing with three very serious sinners and that even his own soul was in peril here. "He is the devil. The devil I tell you. Now who else have you seen with the devil?"

"Lots of people," said Beatrice. "If he's really the devil then I think he's been treated unfairly. He's really quite nice when you get to know him. Licky loves him, and Licky only likes nice people."

"The devil is not a nice person," cried El Gran Inquisitor. "He is the epitome of evil. The father of lies. The prince of serpents. The..."

"Ooh!" Beatrice clapped her hands excitedly. "I didn't know Hiss was a prince. I like him much better than I like the King. The King is grumpy and he wants to hang us."

"He has my sympathies," said El Gran Inquisitor. "Have you ever seen the King with the devil?"

Beatrice shrugged. "Well, yes, in the same room. But not really talking to each other."

"That is enough for me," said El Gran Inquisitor. "Do I have to torture you to make you tell me who else you saw with the devil?"

"No," shuddered Beatrice. "I don't like torture. They say it hurts. I've seen everyone with the devil. All of us. But I still don't think he really is the devil."

"Of course he isn't," snapped Sam.

El Gran Inquisitor sighed. "Oh dear. Well, I have your confessions that you have all consorted with the devil. That is enough for me to authorise your execution. It would be nice though, if you would repent. Tell me, are you sorry you consorted with the devil?"

"Not really," said Beatrice. "I'm sorry, he cooked my Mummy. But I like talking to him. He…"

"That will do. We'll just say you repent. Now, my men are preparing kindling. We are going to set this boat on fire and burn you, your King and all his men and the devil alive, in punishment for your sins. May God have mercy on your souls."

Sam leaped towards El Gran Inquisitor but was clubbed unconscious to the floor by one of the guards. When he awoke, he was tied to a stake on the deck of the Jolly Bloodbath. He looked around, his head throbbing and saw that all his classmates had likewise been tied to stakes, and so had the King, Captains Righteous and Murderer, Dr. Bruit and Hiss and several people he didn't recognise.

Beatrice was sobbing. "Licky? Where's Licky? Where's my Licky?" There was no sign of the little dog.

Sam noticed that the entire deck had been covered with straw and that El Gran Inquisitor stood next to the jolly boats, ready to escape from the vessel as soon as the flames got too high.

"It is my honour, as El Gran Inquisitor of his Catholic Majesty of Spain's Kingdom of Spain, to hereby proclaim sentence of death upon the usurper King George of England for the crime of consorting with the devil. Likewise I also pronounce sentence of death upon the devil himself, also known as Lucifer, Beelzebub and Satan, for being the devil…"

"Excussse me, pleassse," cried Hiss, struggling with his bonds. "My name's Hiss. Hiss sometimes known as foulness, vermin, excrescence, pestilence and vomit, but never as Lucifer, Sssatan or that other feller."

"You're making a terrible mistake if you think you'll get away with this," cried Captain Righteous. "As soon as I get free I will hunt you down like a dog."

Dr. Bruit believed it was time he had his say also. "And I'll pull off your stupid pointy hat and shove it up your..."

"And I'll have your face peeled off and fed to starving children," roared Captain Murderer.

"Empty promises," sneered El Gran Inquisitor. "And now, I must prepare to conquer this Godless kingdom and you must prepare to meet your maker and beg His forgiveness."

He lowered a burning torch to the straw covered deck and turned to his men, ordering them to into the jolly boats at once.

CHAPTER THE NINETEENTH
FIRE! FIRE!

To the children and men and Hiss tied on the deck of the *Jolly Bloodbath*, the Spaniards sounded as if they were having a particularly jolly time in the jolly boats as they rowed back to land, cracking jokes about fire and death and the likelihood of their victims ending up in Limbo, Purgatory or Hell.

Reaching the beach, the still chuckling Spaniards leapt ashore and pulled El Gran Inquisitor's boat up onto the dry sand so that his feet and robes wouldn't get wet as he stepped out. To their surprise he let out a heartfelt sigh.

"Tell me, Defenders of the faith, do you think I was too lenient with those sons of the serpent?"

"Lenient, oh Hugeness?"

"Yes, lenient. Do you not see that by burning them alive ... that is having them die by the flesh being boiled and burnt from their bones ... I have prepared them for their eternal suffering in the Lakes of Boiling Blood in Hell?"

"Hmm..." nodded the Spaniards. "It is indeed a dilemma, Brother of God."

"A dilemma on which I need time to meditate," declared El Gran Inquisitor. "You take the coastal path to our next town of conquest at Flenge. I'll cut across the moorland."

***

Speaking of dilemmas, back on the *Jolly Bloodbath* our heroes and villains and King and Royal Navy were experiencing one of their own. When El Gran Inquisitor had set the straw alight it had popped and crackled and snapped like the finest breakfast cereal. A tremendous smoke had billowed up like a pea soup fog whipping round the deck sending everyone into coughing fits.

"Cof...Cof...At least we won't see our friends burned alive...cof...cof!" spluttered Sam, which observation sent Jolly Roger into a laughing fit to rival his coughing fit. But then...with a sizzle...the fire went out. After a moment the wind turned sending the smoke off deck.

"Cof...What happened? Cof!" asked Katey.

"It's the straw they used," said Captain Righteous. "It must have been wet. That's why it's smoking so much. We're saved. Three cheers for King George!"

"Never mind that now," said the King. "We're still trussed up like guinea-fowl. Say what you will about the Spanish but they certainly know how to tie a good knot." It was true. No matter how much the captives wriggled and wiggled they could find no way to slip out of their bonds.

"Cof! It would help if that blasted hay would stop smoking so much, it's playing havoc with my allergies." grumbled Captain Murderer.

"Speaking of the haysss," said Hiss, "the smokesss warmed it upsss. Look at that lovely sparksss." He was right. The flames had merely gone dormant as the hay warmed itself until it was ready for another blaze. The sparks sparkled and a flame took hold and started creeping across the deck, gaining strength with every inch.

"Here we go again," chuckled Jolly Roger. "Tanning, singeing and roasting coming up!"

"We might be saved yet if the wind turns again and blows the flame out," said Captain Righteous. The wind did turn but only in a direction that served to act as a huge bellows puffing the flames to greater heights.

"That's it, our goose is cooked," snarled Dr. Bruit. "What a way to go."

"Wait!" shouted Sam. "Be quiet! Did you hear that sound?" They turned to where a grappling hook had clattered onto the deck. It skidded back and took purchase against a wooden balustrade.

"Someone's climbing up the side of the ship!" Katey exclaimed.

"Be funny if it's another Spaniard," laughed Jolly Roger. The next second a head appeared over the gunwhale. And it was a Spaniard! But no ordinary Spaniard, for this one wore a Robin the Boy Wonder style mask! The head was attached to a perfectly proportioned body that leaped aboard with a single bound. With a wave of his shoulder length jet black hair, the Spaniard smiled a heart-fluttering smile and bowed low to the prisoners.

"I am..." he declared, pausing for theatrical impact, "...Torres!" Through the building flames he certainly cut a fine figure as he stood hands on hips, with his puffy-sleeved white shirt tucked tightly into scarlet cummerbund over ever so tight black leather trousers which tucked into fold over blue suede knee boots. A rapier completed the picture, hanging from his waist. "Yes, I am Torres, Guardian of the Good, Bamboozler of the Bad! For the past decade in Spain my name has been the byword for Justice. I am the hero of the peasant, the love of all *señoritas*, and the death of all tyrants. I am...Torres!"

"Fascinating but it's getting a little hard to hear you over the roaring of the flames, my dear sir," called Captain Righteous. "What say you cut us loose and we continue your CV over a cup of grog back on dry land?"

"Drink never touches my lips!" declared Torres. "My father was a drunkard and his father before him. But you are right to draw my attention to the job at hand. Now I can either cut you loose and we can swim back to shore or I can put out these flames and save the ship for you. What do you suggest? For I am...Torres! And though I follow my own flag I am a fair man and happy to discuss all sides to a solution."

"Don't mind which as long as you make it snappy," said Captain Righteous who could feel the heat of the flames spreading in his direction.

"Snappy? What is this snappy you speak of?" asked the Spaniard.

"Just get on with saving us and the ship, you heroic haddock!" bawled the already singed Captain Murderer.

"Ahh, yes," said Torres. "On with the show! Now what is the best way to put out a fire? Hmm? I see many options open to me."

"Just select one and go for it," shouted Dr. Bruit, promising himself that he would cut this idiot's head off his shoulders as soon as he was free.

"Well, I'm a bit of a showman," declared Torres. "So I think I shall use my fine rapier to quench the flames." With a flourish he whipped the sword from his waistband and flashed it in a figure eight movement. "Dammit!" he cursed. "This is my number 2 sword. It has a much too thin blade for the business at hand. Wait there, everybody. I'll be back before you know it." Before anyone could utter a word, Torres had leaped back over the side of the

110

ship and the splash of the sea could be heard even over the now roaring flames which were taking a stronghold not only on the hay but also parts of the deck.

"Funny that," chuckled Jolly Roger. "For a minute there I thought he was going to rescue us." The next few minutes were not good minutes in the lives of the captives. What positive things can you say about being burned alive? It's hot. You certainly don't feel the chill or draughts as the flames get closer to your toes. Burning to Death was used as a criminal deterrent for many years in Great Britain and it has to be said that there was a noticeable drop in repeat offenders during the time it was in use. But on the whole it is a horrible way to go, right up there with falling into a volcano or being eaten by a dinosaur. And then the wind changed again. This was not a good thing for now the flames were fanned even faster in the direction of the prisoners. Hair and clothing started to smoke and singe. And then...and then...Torres leapt back on board brandishing a slightly fatter rapier.

"Fear not! You are saved! For I am...Torres!" bawled the hero of the hour over the now roaring flames. "I am the hero of all peasants and the love of all...."

"Shurrup and save us!" screamed the King.

Stirred into action, Torres set to, dancing and prancing, to-ing and fro-ing across the deck, his sword whipping the life out of each and every flame he encountered. He stopped halfway through his work, a worried look upon his face. "This is not a fair fight and Torres is known only for his fairness. And so..." For the rest of the battle Torres used only one leg, hopping madly across the deck in pursuit of each flame. It was a hard-fought war as the wind kept playing a part, reviving the vanquished flames into a fresh onslaught on the beleaguered Spaniard. But

111

eventually all flames were extinguished except for the one travelling up Dr. Bruit's trouser leg.

"Put my pants out!" screamed the Doctor. "Hellllpppp!"

With one final flourish of his wrist, Torres whipped the burning trousers from off Dr. Bruit's legs and hurled them overboard.

"Once again I triumph for I am...Torres!" the Spaniard waved his sword in the air before bowing low, a look of pride on his face. It took his flashing blade but a minute to cut free all prisoners and then, slipping his sword back in his belt he waved a hand and leapt over the edge of the ship shouting, "I go in search of injustice! Remember the name of...Torres!"

CHAPTER THE TWENTIETH
OUT OF THE FIRE AND INTO THE FRYING PAN

Sam looked at Righteous, Righteous looked at Sam, Hiss looked at Captain Murderer and Captain Murderer looked at Katey, who was looking at Beatrice, who was busy looking for Licky.

"Licky! Licky!" she called. "He's probably hiding somewhere. He doesn't like fires."

"Neither do I," chortled Jolly Roger.

"Ahem!" coughed the King, clearing his scorched throat. "Why is everybody standing around looking at each other instead of acting?"

"Acting, Sire?" asked Righteous, thinking that this was neither the time nor the place for play acting, yet loathe to disappoint the King yet again. "By all means. What manner of acting would your highness like to see? Farce perhaps or something a little more highbrow?"

"Dolt!" cried the King. "We don't wish to watch a performance. We wish to see these brigands in irons."

"Brigands, Sire?"

"Yes, brigands, pirates, outlaws, criminals, gallows bait. Call them what you will." He pointed angrily at Sam and Katey. "Clap them in irons and hang 'em."

Righteous bit his lip and frowned. "Really, Sire?"

"Yes, really. Let's be done with them once and for all."

"But Sire," said Righteous. "After all we have been through together. I thought perhaps..."

"Sire, if I may?" said Katey, bobbing a little curtsey. "My friend, Sam was prepared to risk his life to save you, even though you have already condemned us to die."

"So?" said the King. "I'm the King. Of course he was prepared to risk his life to save me. That's his duty. It's your duty. It's everybody's duty. It makes no difference. You are condemned to die, and die you most surely shall."

"But Sire," said Katey. "Surely you have more important things to do. The kingdom has been invaded by strange men who tried to burn us all to death. We could help you defeat them."

The King laughed. "What rot. I am the King. I am the supreme commander of the fleet and the army. I can crush them like that." He clicked his fingers.

"But your fleet and army aren't here," Katey persisted. "We are."

"Not for long," snarled Captain Murderer, grabbing the girl around the neck. "Shall I cut her throat, Highness?"

"No," said the King. "Hang her. Hang them all."

"Licky!" cried Beatrice, pointing out to sea. There on a rock, some distance away, sat Licky, soaking wet, and barking up a storm. "Stay there, Licky. I'm coming to get you!" She dodged through Bruit's legs and flung herself into the ocean.

"Seems like a pretty good idea to me," laughed Jolly Roger. "Who's for an icy dip?" Not waiting for an answer he too jumped overboard, followed by Billy Bones, Sam, Katey and the rest of the crew.

"Don't just stand there!" roared the King. "They are felons. Stop them."

"Er... I don't think we'll have to do that," said Bruit, pointing into the darkness, where several large shapes could be seen moving towards the children.

"What the devil?" cried Righteous.

"It's them sirens, the sea witches," said Murderer. "They'll make short work of 'em."

Sure enough, Queenie and her sisterhood of fishy viciousness were closing in upon the children as they swam to join Licky on the outermost rock of the Devil's Fangs.

"I say, Sire," said Righteous. "Shouldn't we try and rescue them? I mean, it's not really done to leave them at the mercy of sea hags, is it?"

The King shrugged. "Why not? They are condemned to die, and die they shall. Besides, we have a Spanish invasion to quell. Back to shore, boys, once more for Saint Harry and King George."

***

As the King and his followers returned to shore, Queenie and her hideous sirens rounded up the children and prepared to cook them up in a large cast iron cauldron, All the while, Licky ran around barking and snapping at them.

"Oh do be quiet, you wretched beast," cried Queenie. "We're not going to eat you. If you're a good doggy we might even give you some choice left-overs."

As the logs under the pot were lit, Jolly Roger began to laugh. "Ha! Imagine it, twice in one day we find ourselves burned alive. It's not many people can live to boast of that, is it? I wonder what's going to happen to us next."

"Maybe that dashing Torres will come and save us again," said Katey with what sounded suspiciously like a love-lorn sigh.

"Dashing?" said Sam with a sneer. "He was an idiot and he dresses like a girl, with his big frilly shirts."

"He was not an idiot," snapped Katey. "He saved our lives. And I loved his shirt."

"Getting hot isn't it?" giggled Roger as the water around them began to bubble and boil.

"AAA-Choooo!" sneezed Beatrice as Queenie flung a pinch of pepper in her face.

"Excussse me, pleassse, your Prettynesss," said Hiss, who might have been blushing with embarrassment, or maybe his normally greenish face had turned red because of the heat of the flames. "You weren't planning to eat usss without any nice and tassssty herbsss were you?"

"What's it to you?" snapped Queenie, who always got irritable when she was hungry.

"Well, I've got sssome nice ssstar anaisss in my breechesss. You'll find it really bringsss out the flavour."

"Hiss?" said Beatrice, astonished. "Why are you helping them?"

Hiss shrugged. "Well, way I sssseeeessss it isss thisss. We're going to get eaten whether we likesss it or not? Yesss?"

"Yes, so?"

"Well, if we're going to get eaten, I would sssooner people sssay, oh, that Hiss, he tasssted great, than oh, remember that horrible Hisss we ate, wasssn't it disssgusssting?"

Beatrice saw his point. "Yes, that wouldn't be a nice way to be remembered. I suppose you're right."

Hiss began to giggle as Queenie reached a scaly hand into his breeches and pulled out a pouch of mixed herbs and star anais. "How many of these stars, do we need?"

"Two ssshould suffice, your lovelinessss," said Hiss. "And you might want to try a pinch of cumin. That'ssss the brown powder. Not to everybodyssss tassste, but my

116

Captainsss likesss it." He stifled a sob at the memory of happier times.

Queenie flung the herbs and spices into the pot and told her girls to put more logs on the fire. "I'm starving," she grumbled.

"You know, I can't quite make up my mind which is worse, being burned at the stake or being boiled alive," mused Roger, who had stopped laughing and was now sweating profusely into the soup he was standing in.

Just then, there was a sloshing of water and a figure in a sodden white shirt and tight leather breeches pulled himself up onto the Devil's Fangs. He stood for a moment, gasping for breath, before pulling his dazzling rapier from his hip and flourishing it, wildly. "Fear not," he panted. For I am... Torres! Guardian of the Good, Bamboozler of the Bad! The hero of the peasant, the love of all señoritas, and the death of all tyrants. Helper of the helpless, I give succour to the succourless, faith to the faithless. I am...Torres!"

"Hooray!" cheered Katey. "I knew you would save us."

"Save the congratulations til later," sniffed Sam. "We're still cooking and he's got an army of angry sirens to deal with first."

Sam's comment may not have been particularly gracious, but it was true. Queenie, had seen this particular meal snatched from her talons several times already and she was not prepared to allow it to happen again. She was hungry, she was cranky and she was determined to eat. She shrieked like a banshee as she flung herself upon the hapless Spaniard.

"I will eat you raw!" she screeched, clawing at Torres' impossibly handsome face.

"Ah-ah-ah!" Torres admonished her, stepping back, deftly avoiding a patch of slippery seaweed. "Not the face, *señorita*. You would not wish to break the hearts of all the ladies in Christendom, would you?"

"I will eat your face, blast you," cried Queenie. "Girls, get him."

"You know, this reminds me of the time I liberated the harem of Malik the Turk," Torres reminisced happily. "Things did not end well for Malik, but as far as the ladies were concerned, a good time was had by all. Now, one at a time, my lovely *señoritas*. There is plenty of Torres for everybody."

Now, it had been a long time since anyone, except for Hiss (who doesn't really count) had referred to Queenie or her consorts as 'lovely señoritas' and the effect was quite astonishing. For instead of wanting to throw him into the cauldron, the sirens now wanted to kiss him and feel his warm embrace enfold them. Queenie, of course, being Queen, had first dibs and after a mammoth two and a half minute long snog, she eventually allowed Torres to take a short breather.

"Oi!" yelled Sam. "A little help, here."

"One moment, *por favor*," said Torres, before returning his attentions to Queenie, kissing her lips, her cheeks, her gills.

"*Señor* Torres, won't you join us for dinner?" asked Queenie.

"Nothing would delight me more, but alas, I have my figure to think of and I prefer a nice slice of Serrano ham to boiled children. You would like to try it?"

"By all means," said Queenie, who was so hungry she would have eaten boiled leather.

"Then let us release these children and I shall fetch forth a repast fit for such a bevy of beauties," said Torres.

"You heard the man," roared Queenie. "Get those brats out of the cauldron, now!"

The other sirens rushed to obey, tipping the children out of the pot and onto the rocks.

"Thank you, Mr. Torres," sighed Katey, fluttering her eyelashes at her rescuer.

"Hey, you," said Queenie, pinching her arm. "Eyes off. He's mine."

Once the children and Hiss had all been released, Torres removed a leather saddlebag from his shoulder and emptied out a choice ham and a rather sodden looking Spanish omelette, that had crumbled into mush. "It may not look like much, but I assure you it is all *muy deliciosa*."

It is true that Queenie and the Sirens found Torres' Mediterranean diet a little flavourless when compared with their preferred choice of kid stew, but they were all far too polite to say so. The children on the other hand, tucked in with relish. Hiss enjoyed a nice slice of ham, but believed it could do with a dollop of mustard and a little seasoning. Finally, bellies full, Queenie announced her intentions to marry Torres and make him King of the Sirens.

"I am honoured and flattered," smiled Torres, bowing. "But such a marriage would cause mass heartbreak, the like of which this world she have never seen. I cannot give myself to only one, for I am Torres, the love of all *señoritas*..."

Queenie glared at him. "If you don't marry me, then I will eat you and the children. We'll see how much the *señoritas* love you when you've been cooked up and boiled for two and a half hours over a slow flame."

Torres thought about this for a moment. "Ah, you have me, how you say, perched upon the horns of a dilemma. The *señoritas* will break their hearts if I marry and they will break their hearts if I am eaten. It is a rock and a hard place. It is a devil and a deep *azul* sea. It is a problem and that is no exaggeration."

"Well?" said Queenie, staring at him with her fishy eyes.

"It seems I must marry you. But first there is much work to be done. For I came to these shores with a task and I shall not be free to wed until it is accomplished."

"What is it, dearie?" asked Queenie, all sweetness and light now that she had Torres' promise as a *caballero* of the Spanish court. "How can we help?"

"I have a brother. A crazy brother, whose name is dreaded by all. He calls himself El Gran Inquisitor..."

"That freak's your brother?" laughed Jolly Roger. "I might have known."

"Yes, he is my brother. And he is *muy loco*. He wish to recreate the golden age of Spain. To conquer all and bring back the horrors of the Inquisition. Just as the name Torres is a by-word for love and honour and romance and dashing derrin-do, the name of El Gran Inquisitor is a by-word for terror, torture, and ... my English is not so good..."

"No, no, it's perfect," simpered Katey.

"But we get the idea," said Sam, scowling.

"Very well," Torres continued. "He and his followers aim to conquer this country. I aim to stop them. I must depart tonight to help the helpless, to provide succour to the succourless..."

"But what about us?" said Queenie.

"You, my love," said Torres. "You and these brave children shall sail to London down the Thames and save the capital. With luck, I shall have prevailed before my brother reaches there but if not, you must carry on my duty."

"Just a minute," said Katey. "We can't go to London. The King will execute us if he sees us again."

"No," said Sam. "This is our chance to clear our names and save the nation. The King will probably knight us and make us all rich."

"Yesss," agreed Hiss. "Becaussse the King ssseeemsss sssso reasssonable."

"Then may I ask you, my betrothed, to see these brave children safely to London?" asked Torres, stopping to kiss Queenie's clammy hand.

"You may, my sweet."

"Then it is time for me to say *adios*." And with that, Torres, the protector of the peasants, the love of all señoritas and all the rest of it, gave them all a reassuring wink before diving into the water and swimming to shore.

"Well then," said Queenie. "We better get you lot back on board your ship and set sail, eh? Come on girls. We'll give them a push out to sea."

CHAPTER THE TWENTY-FIRST
BY SEA AND LAND

"Midshipman..." mused Midshipman Dunnington. "It's a funny old word. Midshipman." He and Leach had been left on watch to guard the *Jolly Bloodbath* while the King and the rest of the crew had gone ashore in pursuit of the Spaniards. They had chosen the crow's nest as the perfect vantage point to keep an eye on any approaching enemies. This had been a perfect idea until the sea fog eerily stole up and around the ship, limiting vision to six or so feet. Listening to Dunnington blether on about his favourite topic, the meaning of words, had sent Leach into a deep sleep leaning against his blunderbus.

"I wonder what the word is derived from?" Dunnington droned on. "Of course you are aware that a lot of so-called English words are derived from the Latin? Did you know that? Eh, Leachy boy?" Leach just let out a snore in answer. "No, it's true." Dunnington continued undeterred. "Goes back to the Roman conquest of these isles. They didn't just leave Roman walls, bridges and roads behind. They also left words. Roman words. Isn't that fascinating? I never meant to be a midshipman, you know. I don't think midshipman is a Roman word. Doesn't sound like it. No, I was going to be a school teacher. Teacher, now that word comes from the Latin techi, techo, techos, meaning to teach or spread knowledge through learning. 'Ere, what's that?"

That was a bump and a skittering and scattering and skivvering of flab across the main deck. Someone or something had come aboard.

"Is that you, Captain Righteous?" Midshipman Dunnington yelled, leaning over the side of the crow's nest and jerking Leach awake. No answer came apart from a strange slopping sound as though someone or something or things were slorping up the mainmast in their direction.

"Damn this mist!" cursed Leach peering down through the drifting fog. "Can hardly see an arm in front of me."

"Shh! Listen!" said Dunnington. The two men listened. The slorping sound was getting nearer and nearer.

"That's not the Captain," cried Leach, picking up his blunderbus and aiming it downwards towards the approaching sound. Somehow controlling his nerves he waited until the bloodshot green eyes of the first siren appeared through the mist before pulling the trigger. A predominately green technicolour mess exploded in every direction coupled with a banshee scream from Hell.

"One down!" Leach smiled grimly. "Your turn, Dunny!"

Now they might have been in with a fighting chance to protect the crow's nest if Midshipman Dunnington had remembered to bring his own blunderbus up to the nest rather than his dictionary, but he hadn't. And he was loathe to throw his fine dictionary down at the three sirens who were following their sister up the mainmast. And do you know how long it takes to reload a blunderbus? The answer is an easy one. Too long. Within the time it takes you to peel a hard-boiled egg, the sirens had overcome, boiled and peeled Midshipman Dunnington and Seaman Leach and taken over the *Jolly Bloodbath*.

"Hooray and Ha-Ha!" cheered and chuckled Jolly Roger as the two peeled skulls crashed to the deck at his feet. "On to London!"

****

You will remember that we left El Gran Inquisitor about to cut off across the heather and moorland on route to Flenge. Strange then to find him completely naked, drying himself off at the sea's edge in the shadows of the cliffs under Bollingbrook Hall. From behind a boulder he pulled out and donned his glorious robes, tucking his hood to align the eye holes perfectly in place.

"That's better. I feel myself again. No more doubts. No more self-questioning. I am the tool of *El Señor*. When His voice speaks to me in my head, I obey." He sat on the boulder and waited and sure enough *El Señor* spoke to him in his head.

"Crackkkkle...fzzzz...blllpppp..." It wasn't the best connection. The cliffs around him were obviously playing havoc with the signal.

"My dear Spanish onion, I am so proud of you!" Ah, here we go. *El Señor's* coming in loud and clear now thought El Gran Inquisitor. "In my loving and forgiving name I want you to kill anyone who isn't an adherent of the true faith or a Spaniard. Go to London and proclaim yourself Holy Protector of Britain. Oh, and by the way, kill your brother, Torres. He ees a pain in the ass! Over and out!"

"Torres!" snarled El Gran Inquisitor beneath his hood. "I should have strangled him with my umbilical cord in our Mother's womb when I had the chance. But it will come to pass for it is the will of *El Señor*. And now...to Flenge!"

CHAPTER THE TWENTY SECOND
A NAUTICAL WEDDING

The British Isles were under direct threat from a foreign power. The forces of El Gran Inquisitor had already landed and the King's person was in danger. Sam knew that speed was of the essence if they were to save the country. He knew that their best hope lay in reaching London before the invaders and alerting the authorities to the danger that faced them. You can imagine then his frustration during that long voyage from the Devil's Fangs in Cornwall to Southend and the mouth of the River Thames. Yes, it is true that they had the help of the sirens to guide them, but the sirens were no better sailors than Sam or his classmates. After two days' at sea they finally came in sight of land, disembarked and raced ashore, telling everyone on the beach that the Spanish were coming and to take up arms as fast as they could. Instead of the locals doing as they were told they stared at them uncomprehendingly and muttered things like *"Sacre bleu, Alors* and *Mon Dieu!"* Yes, the Sirens had taken a wrong turning in the fog and brought them across the Channel to Calais.

After a brief stop to take on board much needed provisions and to take advantage of the special offers in the Duty Free shop, they sailed away again and five weeks later, after a brief stop-over in Klöst, a much neglected beauty spot off the coast of Norway, they finally reached

Southend and began the last leg of their journey up the River Thames.

During those five weeks, the crew had got to know the Sirens reasonably well and Hiss, who realised that his love for Queenie was always going to remain unrequited, had turned his attentions to her equally repulsive hand-maiden Betty. Betty, who had lived a sheltered life, found Hiss quite cute.

"Betty, will you make me the happiessst creature in the world and be my bride?" he asked as they approached Southend.

"Okay," said Betty, who had never been proposed to before and thought it might be quite fun being married to a pirate.

Queenie gave her blessing and the crew and sirens alike all decided to weigh anchor for the night to celebrate the wedding in style.

"Have we really got time for this?" asked Sam. "Couldn't we put the wedding off until after we save the country?"

Katey disagreed. "It's been five weeks since we saw El Gran Inquisitor. He's probably taken over the country by now and if he hasn't then one more night won't make any difference."

"Pleasssse, SSssssam," pleaded Hiss. "I'll be your besssst friend."

Sam shuddered. "Thanks, Hiss."

"Oh, go on," said Beatrice. "I've never been to a wedding before and I want to be a bridesmaid. Can we stop off at the shops and get a special dress? I want to wear blue. Do you like blue, Betty?"

"It's okay," said Betty.

"Oh, goodie," said Betty. "And Licky is going to be best man, aren't you, Licky?" Licky licked Beatrice and then licked Hiss, before turning his attentions to licking his own bottom.

"Licky isss going to be the bessst bessst mansss ever," sighed Hiss, happily.

Katey and Beatrice went ashore to find a bridesmaid's dress for Beatrice. It took longer than they had hoped. While Southend was full of shops selling fishing tackle and bait, there was only one dress shop in the entire town and that was closed for refurbishment.

Beatrice began to cry tears of bitter disappointment. "It's not fair! I don't ask for much, just a pretty blue dress for me and a blue lace collar for Licky. It's not fair."

At last, a window above the shop opened and an old woman peered out at them. "What's all that racket?" she demanded.

"Sorry to disturb you," said Katey. "But we're going to a wedding and my friend needs a dress."

"Tough. We're closed for refurbishment. Go away." The woman slammed the window shut and Beatrice began to howl. Licky, who had joined them also began to howl. At length the window opened again. "Okay, okay! I'll get you a dress," yelled the old woman.

"Oh, goodie!" screamed Beatrice. She began tap dancing around the street and singing about the birds and the crickets getting married on the morrow.

Beatrice didn't stop singing all the time the old lady was measuring her and fitting her out in a gown of blue silk. "I think I'm in heaven," she sighed.

At last, the gown was ready and Licky was proudly wearing his brand new collar.

"That will be fifteen guineas," said the old lady.

"Oh." Beatrice's face fell.

"We don't have any money," said Katey. "We've got a couple of bottles of rum and some ship's biscuits, if that's any good?"

The old lady's face grew stern. "Wasting my time? I'm going to call the yeoman of the guard. He'll clap you both in prison. Now get out of that dress, you dirty little beggar girl."

Beatrice began to cry again.

"Don't do it, Beatrice," said Katey, brandishing a pistol. "This lady isn't going to charge us a thing."

They fled the shop, as quickly as they could and made their way back to the *Jolly Bloodbath*.

"We could get into trouble for that," said Beatrice.

"I know," said Katey.

"Would you really have shot her if she hadn't given us the dress?"

"No," laughed Katey. "The pistol isn't loaded. Look!" She aimed into the air and pulled the trigger. There was a loud bang and a seagull fell dead at her feet. "Oh... errr...."

Beatrice burst into tears. "Poor little birdy," she cried. "He wasn't hurting anyone. He..."

"Shhh," said Katey. "You can take him back to the ship and we can give him a proper burial at sea. How does that sound?"

"Horrible," sobbed Beatrice. "You would have killed that woman. You are just as bad as Captain Murderer and Dr. Bruit. I hate you. I hate you. I hate you."

"But Beatrice, it was an accident," cried Katey. "Look, I'll throw the gun away. I wish I'd never set eyes on it." She tossed the gun over her shoulder and as it landed it discharged yet again, this time killing the yeoman of the guard who had been trying to sneak up on the robbers and catch them.

The girls and the little dog ran to the jolly boat and rowed at full speed back to the *Jolly Bloodbath*. They were just climbing aboard when Beatrice burst into tears again and wanted to go back to shore, where they could see a group of angry men waving clubs at them.

"We need to go back and get Mr. Seagull. You promised we could bury him at sea," she sobbed.

"Don't worry," said Katey, who was trembling with shock. "I'm sure those nice men will give him a decent funeral. And it's better that way, they probably knew Mr. Seagull better than we did."

"That's true," said Beatrice, wiping her eyes and doing a twirl on the deck. "Look everyone, look at my dress. Look how it swirls around me like a swirly thing."

"We'll have to postpone the wedding," said Katey. "I... I killed a man."

"And a seagull," said Beatrice. "It was horrible. She's gone mad. She's worse than Captain Murderer."

"No one isss worssse than my Captainsss," said Hiss, feeling strangely protective of his former master.

"What happened?" asked Sam.

Beatrice and Katey told them everything.

"You should have brought the dead man back to the ship for the wedding feast," said Queenie.

"And the sssseagull," said Hiss.

"Yes, it won't be much of a wedding without any dead people to eat," sniffed the blushing bride.

"I'm a murderer," said Katey. "I... I should turn myself in. If I stay here I'll only get you into trouble."

"No," said Sam. "You made a mistake. You didn't mean to kill anyone."

"Small comfort for the dead guy," laughed Roger.

"And Mr. Seagull," said Beatrice.

"Listen," said Sam. "Like it or not, we're outlaws now. We're pirates. We have different rules to most people. Yes, Katey made a mistake. But she's learned her lesson. Let that be enough."

"What lesson hasss she learned?" asked Hiss.

"Not to play with guns," said Sam. "They're dangerous."

And let that be a lesson to you too, gentle reader. Don't play with guns, especially not with real guns. They have a nasty habit of having bullets in them even when you think they don't.

"Err... guys," said Barry Eckles, a quiet lad, who had been placed on watch duty. "There's a group of angry looking men with guns, rowing towards us."

It was true.

"Ahoy!" shouted the angriest man in the boat. "We've come to apprehend a murderess."

"I should go," said Katey. "I killed that man. I deserve to be punished."

"Nonsense," snorted Queenie. "I've killed thousands of men and I've never been punished. Everything happens for a reason my girl. You leave this to us." She turned to the rest of the sirens. "Ready, ladies?"

"You bet!" cried the ladies, flopping off the deck and into the sea.

Within moments the little rowing boat and the angry men with guns had disappeared beneath the surface of the sea. Minutes later, a couple of bones floated to the surface, to be followed soon after by a crowd of happy and well-fed sirens.

"There, see?" said Queenie. "I told you these things happen for a reason. We just got our wedding feast and you're still free. It all turned out nice in the end."

"She's not wrong there," laughed Jolly Roger.

***

The wedding itself came as a bit of an anti-climax. Apart from the fact that the ceremony itself was conducted according to Siren law and took place under water and Hiss, Licky and Beatrice almost drowned, it was a fairly dull affair. Once the vows had been said and the registry book signed and the speeches made, Sam called everyone to attention. "Time to set sail, me hearties. We've got a kingdom to save."

And so it was that the crew of the *Jolly Bloodbath* raised the anchor and entered the Thames Estuary, for the final leg of its journey.

CHAPTER THE TWENTY THIRD
HEROES, VILLAINS, ETHICS AND UNWRITTEN RULES

Now, storytelling is not quite so straight forward as some of you have no doubt been led to believe. Yes, there is a written rule that a story should have a beginning, a middle and an end, though there is also an unwritten rule that states that it doesn't always follow that the story has to proceed in that order. Don't worry, we aren't going to skip back to the beginning now, and we're certainly not going to jump forward to the end either; that's the beauty of unwritten rules, you can ignore them sometimes and if anyone pulls you up on them you can always say you never knew about it because you'd never seen it written anywhere. Yes, it is easy for us to ignore the unwritten rule about having our beginning come after our ending, but there are some other unwritten rules that are much harder to ignore. Take for example the case of Katey Cross. As we have seen, she has just shot an innocent yeoman of the guard and a seagull. Yes, it was an accident, but even so, one of the unwritten rules of literature and storytelling in general is that our heroes and heroines don't kill innocents and if they do, then it is the author's duty to make sure they are suitably punished for it. Otherwise, some more impressionable readers may get it into their heads that it is quite acceptable to go around shooting people and we can't have that. Yes, some of you may find it unfair, but Katey Cross will have to be punished for her deeds, and believe me, she will be punished, in our own good time. Of course, while we are thinking up a suitable punishment, please feel free to raise the argument that while a hero or heroine is not at liberty to go around killing people willy-nilly, a villain can kill as many people as he or she feels like. Captain Murderer has killed countless numbers of innocents, as has his dear brother Dr. Bruit. El Gran Inquisitor may not have actually killed anyone yet in these pages, but he has certainly tried to, and the sirens.... well, popular opinion is divided on the subject of sirens. Yes, it's true that they have formed an uneasy alliance with Sam, Katey and the crew of the *Jolly Bloodbath*, and it is true that they have killed more than their fair share of innocents and not so innocents, but then again, they fall into a completely different category. They aren't really heroes or heroines, but they aren't out and out villains either, they're monsters and monsters have their own set of rules both written and unwritten.

Anyway, we digress, you've been warned, Katey Cross will be punished for carelessly shooting people and seagulls but as to the manner of punishment, you'll just have to wait and see. Just bear in mind that so far, while the death count in these pages has been high, nobody of much consequence has been killed to date, and another of those pesky unwritten rules states that all good stories need to pull on the heart strings by ruthlessly murdering at least one of the characters we have come to know and care about.

***

The Jolly Bloodbath made good speed as it sailed up the Thames towards London and spirits on board were high. Hiss and Betty viewed the voyage as a honeymoon and spent most of their time, smooching in the crow's nest or frolicking in the water, laughing and giggling like love's young dream. Beatrice refused to take off her new dress after the wedding and was still happily dancing around the deck in blue, singing "I'm the prettiest girl in the whole wide world," over and over. Sam was eager for adventure and the chance to clear his name and be a hero and Katey believed that if she helped to save the nation from El Gran Inquisitor then maybe she would be able to forget about that unfortunate business with the pistol and the yeoman of the guard and the seagull. Queenie was also in good spirits because with each passing hour she believed that she was getting closer and closer to her beloved Torres, who was no doubt out there somewhere, risking life and limb in defence of the defenceless.

"You know, it's funny," chuckled Roger, looking out over the river. "But I was expecting to see everything in ruins. Isn't that what invading armies do? Burn and destroy stuff?"

Sam nodded his head in agreement. "Yes, you're right. By all accounts the whole country should be in flames. Maybe we really are in time. Maybe El Gran Inquisitor hasn't got here yet."

"I hope not," said Katey. "It's got to be us who saves the day, not the army or navy. It's the only way we can clear our names."

Roger began laughing again. "I love these choices we get. We either get hacked to pieces in battle by crazy guys with hooded masks or we get taken prisoner by them and tortured and burned at the stake again, or the King has us all hanged for pirates. Ah well, at least we won't die of boredom, eh, Sammy?"

At last, as night fell over London, the *Jolly Bloodbath* docked, with help from Hiss and the sirens beside the Tower of London. They had hoped to land somewhere a little less conspicuous, but the river was filled with all manner of ships and they had to take the only space available.

"That's funny," said Sam. "It looks as if the whole British Navy is moored here."

"Who cares?" said Beatrice. "I want to get ashore and show everyone my pretty dress. Come on Hiss, we're going to have lots of fun. I've always wanted to go shopping in London."

"No thankssss," said Hiss. "Hissss hatessss ssshhhopping. Hisss wants to stay here with Betty."

"You're no fun anymore," sniffed Beatrice. "You just want to spend all your time with your boring old wife."

"Watch it, girly," snapped Betty. "I'm not too old to take you over my knee and bite your head off."

"Do you want us to come with you?" Queenie asked Sam.

Sam thought about this for a moment. It would certainly be handy to have a gang of super powered monsters on his side, but at the same time, he doubted very much if London was ready for the sirens yet. He didn't want to cause complete panic. "No, you better stay here at the river and guard the ship for us. We shouldn't be too long." He turned to the rest of his crew. "Come on gang, let's go raise an army and give El Gran Inquisitor a right good kicking."

As they disembarked, they found a group of sailors waiting for them on the quay-side. "What's the big idea?"

136

asked one. "You can't just park that thing here. It's a health and safety hazard."

"We've come to avert a health and safety hazard," said Katey. "The King is in danger and so is the entire country. We need to speak with whoever's in charge."

The sailors weren't impressed. "Oh yeah? The King's in danger is he? And you lot are gonna save him? Bless us, I've heard some rubbish in my time."

"Just take us to whoever's in charge, will you? This is an emergency," snapped Sam.

"Alright, alright, keep your hair on," sighed the sailor. "Hand over your weapons to Big Bill, here."

Sam, Katey and the others did as they were told, handing over swords, daggers and pistols to the aptly named Big Bill, a huge bear of a man with a face like a badly chiselled piece of rock. They were then led up the steps from the quayside and into the Tower of London itself.

"So who is in charge here?" asked Sam as they walked down a dimly lit corridor.

"You'll find out," said one of the sailors.

Finally they came to a large set of double doors guarded by two men in armour. After a whispered consultation with the sailors, the guards opened the doors and announced their presence.

"A gang of dirty kids who reckon we're in a state of emergency."

Sam and the others blinked in the dazzling light from a thousand candles as they entered the main hall of the Tower. There at the far end, seated upon a purple throne, was the last man they had wanted to see. He stared at them from under a purple hood and then began to laugh.

"Bwa-ha-ha! How is it you say? All the things that are nice will be coming into the hands of the man who must wait? Is that it? Welcome, witches. I see El Gran Inquisitor must burn you all over again. How very, very nice."

CHAPTER THE TWENTY-FOURTH
TORTURE - THOSE IN FAVOUR PUT YOUR HANDS UP. OH, YOU DON'T HAVE ANY HANDS TO PUT UP.

Those of you who have visited the Tower of London on school trips or during the Summer hols will know it to be a fun place to wander round. You will have seen the crown jewels (if you could be bothered queuing long enough), Henry VIII's ridiculous suit of armour with built-in foot-long compartment for his grotesque willy, the various spots where hundreds of innocent people were executed or burnt alive, the fun souvenir shop, and all within walking distance of the nearest MacDonald's for the appetite you built up to eat cooked flesh. And then you can go home to watch the telly. It wasn't like that in the Old Days in which our story is set. No souvenir shop, no MacDonalds and no telly. Just the horrible bits.

"I'm terrified," admitted Katey, staring at Henry VIII's armour. They had been bunged into the holding bay that had once been Lady Jane Grey's cell back in the good old days. It had been used as a storeroom for the last few years with all sorts of knick-knacks from down the ages making it a very tight squeeze for our piratical children. "We've had so many deadly adventures already that you would think I'd be used to it by now but I'm more frightened than ever."

"Aw, come on," chuckled Jolly Roger giving Henry VIII's penis a clanging whack with a silver candlestick he'd found in the assorted jumble littering the room. "I mean, what's the worst that might happen?"

"We'll be burned at the stake," replied Katey.

"Ha-Ha! You got me there!" laughed Roger. "Been there, done that, got the T-shirt. Now, look on the bright side. We've always wanted to visit the Tower of London and we all got in without paying. Look at all this fab stuff." He picked up a chunky rosary that had belonged to a long dead martyr and tried to pull it over his head but the string broke sending the shiny beads scattering in all directions. "Catch them! They're so pretty!" Roger went down on his hands and knees to try and scoop up the beads but he was too late as most of them disappeared down a crack in the paved floor. "Help me pull this stone up!"

Sam and Katey and Roger all gripped the stone and were surprised to find it swing aside quite easily. They all gasped as they looked down into a black pit that had been revealed.

"There's a staircase!" cried Katey. "We might be able to escape...again!"

"Better than waiting here to be cooked!" said Sam, leading the way down into the dark.

***

El Gran Inquisitor hadn't burned our crew on the spot because he wanted to savour the moment as part of the celebrations he was lining up after the first Spanish Conquest of England. For the past few weeks he had been forced to work without many of the tools of his trade that had been left behind in his torture chambers under St. Rosana's Holy Church of the Bleeding Feet of Our

Saviour back in Cartagena. Imagine his delight on taking over the Tower of London and finding a suite of rooms designed specifically for tearing apart the living human body in ways he had only dreamed of until now. He hadn't been this happy since boiling his uncle, a heretic, in acid back when he was a boy of eight years of age. He had known then that he would dedicate his life to bringing the love of *El Señor* to the world by slaughtering all those who misinterpreted the holy writings within the good book. England had led the world in methods of torture for centuries at this point in our timeline. Be thankful that we have long given up such cruel ways in the interrogation of our assumed enemies. The worst they will get today is a touch of waterboarding, which never hurt anyone, and a humiliating photo of themselves in the nude being laughed at by a squad of our soldiers. Luxury compared to what is about to go down in our story.

"Beautiful, just beautiful..." muttered El Gran Inquisitor, pulling a steel hoop surmounted by jagged shards of glass from a shelf. He didn't know its name but he could imagine at least ten uses for such a tool. "Oh and look at that rack!" Tears came to his eyes and dribbled out of the holes in his hood as he ran a hand over the world's most tongue-loosening piece of apparatus. "I can picture that Beatrice girl on here. I do hope she doesn't crack too early in proceedings." He uttered the word crack with some relish as though picturing Miss Bollingbrook-Drivelington splitting at the seams. "And as for this...OW!" El Gran Inquisitor had made the mistake of picking up a *Crankle*. This was the actual device used by Cain in the Bible when he realised that the brick hadn't quite finished off his brother Abel. It had been put on the Earth on the ninth day after creation when God decided that mankind needed some kind of slaughtering device to keep the population to a manageable size on such a small world. It had worked wonders for centuries and there is talk of reintroducing it into the Twenty-First Century as overcrowding becomes more and more of a problem. But it was a deadly device as El Gran Inquisitor found when it cleanly sliced off two fingers off his left hand at a single touch. His eyes gleamed with awe at the bloodied instrument as he quickly shoved his maimed hand into a fiery torch to try and fuse the bleeding finger stumps. "Perfection! Absolute perfection. I am in Heaven."

***

"I am in Hell!" chortled Jolly Roger. "I've never told you all how much I hate the dark and cramped areas, have I?" Having pulled the paving stone back into place above them, the crew of Bruit Academy truants were descending in the pitch dark down a narrow, winding staircase that seemed to stretch into the bowels of the earth itself. After the first hundred steps, Roger had dropped the crucifix which had seemingly fallen and fallen and fallen and fallen to neverending depths for there came no sound of it reaching the bottom of the pit they found themselves climbing down.

"I'm sure we'll get to the bottom soon," said Katey after the next 998 steps. But she was wrong she decided after a further 3,567 steps.

"How can there be so many steps without us reaching the other side of the planet?" muttered Sam.

"Or Hell," laughed Roger.

"No, Hell is back up there with El Loco Inquisitor," said Katey. "At least we are getting further away from him with every step. Come on, keep going!"

***

"Idiot! Idiot! Idiot!" It was King George speaking. For the past week, since the fall of London, he had been chained to a wall in the Bloody Tower next to Captain Righteous who was similarly bound. "How can you have let a bunch of tuppenny-halfpenny Spaniards take over my realm?"

"With all due respect, your majesty, we were outclassed and out-played on the day." Righteous responded.

"Out-played? It's not a bloody football match. It's supposed to be war to the death. What are you doing still alive?"

"I can only apologise for still breathing, your royal highness. I shall rectify that mistake at the earliest opportunity."

"Cut it out!" came a voice from outside the tower window. Captain Righteous and the King found their spirits reviving as in through the narrow slot swung the man known as Torres. "The battle isn't over until the battle is over," he said, stating the obvious. "And with Torres on your side the battle is as good as won. For I am Torres..." While Torres repeated his full credentials, Righteous noticed that blood was seeping from the fingers of the glove on his left hand.

***

"We must be at the bottom by now!" said Jolly Roger with what sounded like an almost false laugh. Our crew were truly worn to the bones. They had given up counting the number of steps they had taken at 12,598 at least two hours previously.

"Wait!" said Katey, stopping so abruptly that everyone else stumbled into her. The sound came again, a grating noise before light flooded down upon them. Blinking against the light they saw five Spanish soldiers grinning evilly down at them.

"So you found the Tower of London's famous Steps to Nowhere?" laughed one of the ugly bunch.

Katey, Sam and the others looked downwards as sunlight beamed into the hole. Now they could see that the staircase they had been following was built in a huge loop that went nowhere but back to where it began. The sunlight withered away about fifty feet down the pit in the centre of the steps.

"Up you come," shouted the Spaniard. "You've had enough exercise for one day. Come. It is time to prepare for martyrdom."

CHAPTER THE TWENTY FIFTH
EL GRAN DECEPCIÓN

"I just don't get it," complained Henry Pelham, the Prime Minister of His Majesty's government. "Something smells distinctly fishy to me."

"Aye, well, that's what yer get for building the Tower so close to the river," explained Captain Murderer, as the two men walked across the courtyard of the Tower of London. "It always gets a bit niffy when the tide goes out."

"No," sighed Pelham. "I mean the King. What's he playing at? He's been acting very strange of late. Don't you agree?"

"Not for me to say, sir," said Murderer, reaching discretely for his dagger.

"What I mean to say is this, His Majesty has been behaving very oddly ever since his return to the capital."

"Has he? I hadn't noticed," said Murderer.

"Well, you haven't known him for as long as I have," said Pelham. "I mean, why does he insist on wearing that strange hood all the time? Why does he speak with a funny accent? Why has he promoted you, a stranger, as his Chief Advisor? And why has he sacked the household guard and replaced them with all these Spaniards?"

Captain Murderer sighed. "It's simple, really. It's all part of what he calls *'El Gran Decepcion'*."

"Eh?" asked the Prime Minister.

"That's foreign speak for 'the big deception'," explained Captain Murderer.

"Oh. I see," said the Prime Minister, clearly not seeing. "But who is he deceiving?"

"Everybody," Murderer replied. "He's bringing confusion to his enemies."

The Prime Minister thought about this for a while. "But he's bringing confusion to me too."

Captain Murderer removed his dagger and began picking his teeth with it. "Then perhaps you are one of his enemies?" he said, with a twinkle in his eye.

"Err... no... it's just... you have to admit, it is confusing."

"Not to me it ain't," said Murderer. "It's simple. His Majesty has uncovered a plot by a foreign power to kill him. Therefore, he's going about in disguise. He's heard that there are traitors everywhere, so he's replaced his old advisors with me, and his old guard with new ones."

"Yes, but why Spaniards?"

"Because his Majesty is entering into an alliance with Spain and this seemed like a good way of showing good faith."

"Oh. Well, I'd like to see the King in person please, we really need to discuss this in detail," said the Prime Minister.

"Of course," said Murderer, grinning. "Follow me, his Majesty is waiting for you."

***

The last few weeks had been exceptional for both Captain Murderer and Dr. Bruit. Ever since that night on the outskirts of Flenge, when that ninny Captain Righteous had laid an ambush for El Gran Inquisitor and his men. Yes, things had been going well for Righteous. He had raised an army of peasants that far outnumbered the Spaniards and the invasion would have been over before it had begun if not for some quick thinking on the part of Bruit and Murderer. As Captain Righteous ordered the Spaniards to lower their swords, Murderer had crept up behind the King and pressed his cutlass to his throat, while Bruit had done the same to Righteous. The tables had been well and truly turned and the King had no option but to surrender to El Gran Inquisitor. El Gran Inquisitor had then rewarded Murderer and Bruit by making the brothers his Chief Brothers in Terror.

It was on that first night together that the brothers had witnessed El Gran Inquisitor having one of his many Divine Visitations. These Divine Visitations weren't really much to look at, consisting mainly of El Gran Inquisitor twisting around and shaking and talking to himself and giggling like a lunatic. However, once finished, El Gran Inquisitor had confided in them that he had been instructed to abandon his plans for a military conquest and instead to accomplish his means by subterfuge. Murderer hadn't understood the word, but Bruit had told him it was just another word for 'deception.'

"*Exactamente*," laughed El Gran Inquisitor. "*El Gran Decepcion*. We shall rule this country. I shall pretend to be King George. After all, when we wear a hood, we all look the same. Who is to say I am not the King?"

"Won't people get suspicious?" asked Bruit. "When they hear you speak?"

"How do you mean?" El Gran Inquisitor had asked. "Are you insinuating that my English is not as good as the King's?"

"No, not at all. It's better than the King's," said Bruit. "But your voice is different, that's all."

El Gran Inquisitor had laughed at that. "Of course. It is the hood that changes the voice. Were I to remove my hood, you would be astonished by how different my voice is. We can fool everybody. We shall bring this false king and his men to London as prisoners and dispose of them at our leisure."

"Why not kill 'em now?" asked Murderer, who was looking forward to repaying the King and Righteous for the keel hauling they had given him.

"Because I like to take my time when it comes to administering death," said El Gran Inquisitor. "It is instructive and fun too."

"Alright," said Murderer. "But if they escape, don't say I didn't warn you."

"I won't," promised El Gran Inquisitor. "If they escape, I shall have you boiled in oil and have your head dipped in tar and placed on a spike."

"Oh, right," said Murderer, beginning to wonder for the first time if he had perhaps made a mistake in betraying the King and allying himself with this hooded monster.

***

Yes, things had gone well since their arrival in London. Apart from a few uncomfortable questions, most people had fallen for the big deception and believed that if the King wanted to go around wearing a silly pointy hood,

148

then that was his royal prerogative. The only fly in the ointment, so to speak, was Henry Pelham, the Prime Minister, who was an old-fashioned sort who believed that the only thing that a King should wear upon his head was a crown, and maybe, on occasion a wig, but most definitely not a pointy hood. He meant to have it out with the King that very day, once and for all and hoped that once the King put away his robes and hoods, then they could return once again to managing the realm. He waited impatiently, outside the White Tower for his audience with King George.

"I don't understand it," he kept on saying to himself. "Why on earth would his majesty want to set up home here? He never liked the place. Too many ravens for one thing..." A squadron of ravens swooped overhead and splattered him with poo, before heading off, cawing their little heads off with delight. At last, Captain Murderer returned, red-faced and out of breath. "Well?" said the Prime Minister.

"Well, what?" asked Murderer.

"The King! Can he see me?"

"No. He's gone out."

"Gone out?" The Prime Minister was astonished. "Where's he gone?"

Captain Murderer shrugged. His guess was that he was no doubt torturing one of the numerous prisoners housed in the tower, but he didn't think that would go down well with the Prime Minister, who frowned on such things. "He's gone for a pint."

"Gone for a pint?" Henry Pelham couldn't believe his ears.

"Yeah. Had a rare thirst on him, he did. So he's gone to the pub. I'd come back later in the week if I were you."

"But... but... he's the King of England. He can't just go off to the pub, whenever the fancy takes him."

"Why not?" asked Murderer, genuinely confused. "He's the King, ain't he? Who's gonna stop him?"

"But... he's got papers to sign..." The Prime Minister brandished a pile of papers under Murderer's nose.

"So what? You sign 'em. He won't mind."

"I... but..."

"Look, I'm the King's new adviser, right? Well then, I'll advise him to let you sign 'em. Okay?"

"Errrr... yes... but."

"Right, well, if that's it, I'm off to the bog, for a poo," said Captain Murderer, breaking another unwritten rule, which states clearly that characters in novels, be they heroes or villains, never, ever go to the toilet (unless of course, the novel is about war in the Far East and the characters are suffering from dysentery, in which case it is permitted to mention their toilet habits in a roundabout manner). However, we would like to assure you that Captain Murderer wasn't really going for a poo, he only said he was in order to shock the straight-laced Prime Minister. In reality he was going to his quarters to enjoy a *siesta*, one of the less harmful habits he had picked up from his new Spanish companions.

***

The Prime Minister was left to find his own way to the nearest exit, and if he had chanced to look up, he would have seen three distant figures, edging their way down a rope from the topmost window of the Tower.

"I don't like heights," complained King George, as a gust of wind blew the three men backwards and forwards across the walls of the tower. "And I don't like the wind. Isn't there an easier way out of this place?"

"Ees not so hard," said Torres. "Ees merely a case of the mind of the matter. I tell you how I, Torres, champion of the impoverished, deals with such things. My arms they ees tired and so I say me to my arms, 'arms, you are not tired', and so my mind he triumphs over the matter, no? Ees easy, try it."

"What is he blithering on about, Righteous?" asked the weary King.

"I think what he is trying to say is that if you tell your arms they aren't tired, then they won't be," said Righteous. "It takes some practice... but... gasp.... it seems to work for me, sire."

"Rot!" gasped the King. "I've got blisters on my fingers and don't tell me to try telling my fingers that they don't hurt, or I'll have you hung, drawn and quartered for treason."

They had reached a window on the floor below their cell and Torres clung to the window ledge for a moment before pulling himself inside. When the King and Righteous were about to do the same, he poked his head out of the window and shook it vigorously.

"No, no, no, no, no. What are you doing? You can not come in here. It ees dangerous. *Muy, muy peligroso*."

"So's hanging from a rope at the top of the Tower of London," gasped Righteous.

"*Si*, I know these," agreed Torres. "That ees why, I, Torres, love of all señoritas, friend of the friendless, light of the lightless, succour of the succourless am about to find a different way of escape. But first I must, how you say, check that the coast she ees all clear. No?" Torres, disappeared into the chamber, leaving the King and Righteous dangling from the rope outside the window.

"Well, of all the nerve," complained King George. "I don't see why we couldn't go with him."

"We are unarmed, Sire," explained Righteous. "I suggest we place our trust in the Spaniard. For the moment, at least."

"Hmm, very well, but if I fall and break my neck, I shall hold you both responsible."

***

Hiss and Betty were enjoying the view from the top of the crow's nest on the *Jolly Bloodbath*. "That lookssss like the King, hanging from that window," he said, turning to give his new bride a slimy kiss behind the gills.

"I don't like the King," sniffed Betty. "He was very rude to us."

"Hisss not like him much either," agreed Hiss. "Look, there'ssss that Sssspanishhh windbag Torressss, climbing in a window."

"Torres?" came a voice from the deck. It was Queenie. "My beloved Torres? Where?"

By the time she had slithered up the mast, Torres had disappeared inside the window of the tower, but the King and Captain Righteous were still dangling in mid-air.

"I've a good mind to aim our cannons at them," said Queenie. "That would be a good laugh."

It was then that another head popped out of the window. This one was wearing a large pointy hood. Hiss began to tremble with fear. "Eek! It's El Gran Inquisssitor. He'ssss a bad 'un. Look! He'ssss dragging the King and the other feller inssside."

Hiss was telling the truth. As Queenie stared through the telescope, she saw El Gran Inquisitor haul the King and his companion through the window and into the tower.

"Sssserves them right," laughed Hiss. "He'll probably burn them."

Queenie laughed too but then stopped and frowned. "Just a minute. If he's just captured the King and he's going to burn them. That means he must have captured my lovely Torrey-worrey-woo. What if he hurts him? What if he hurts his lovely, dreamy face? What if he cuts his lovely dreamy hair?"

"He won't cut it, Highnesssss," said Hiss, helpfully. "He'll burn it off. El Gran Inquissssitor likesss firessss."

"Noooooo!" wailed Queenie. "We have to save him. We have to save my lovely jubbly Torrey-worrey."

CHAPTER THE TWENTY SIXTH
SCHOOL REUNION

Now, the last time we saw Sam, Katey, Beatrice and the others, they were being led away by a troop of Spanish guards to prepare for martyrdom. These preparations took the form of a meeting with Dr. Bruit whose new duties, apart from taking on the role of trainee torturer for El Gran Inquisitor, also included that of Tailor of the Damned, an exclusive position in the new regime. It was up to the Tailor of the Damned to make sure that all condemned heretics and political prisoners looked presentable for their execution. This meant measuring the prisoners and then tailoring bespoke 'shifts' for each one to wear on the occasion of their execution. It must be confessed that at first Dr. Bruit was completely ignorant as to what a 'shift' was exactly, but a quick word with one of the Spanish torturers, who also happened to speak exceedingly good English, informed him that a 'shift' was another word for a sheet. These sheets had to reach below the knee but could not trail upon the ground. Ideally, a first-rate shift should fall just three inches above the ankle. Likewise, the sleeves should come to an end three inches above the wrist.

When the children were led into the Fitting Room of the Damned, they tried their best not to show any fear as they caught sight of Dr. Bruit, standing beside the narrow window and squinting as he attempted to thread a large needle.

"We're for it now," giggled Jolly Roger. "He's gonna stitch us up good and proper this time."

Katey nudged him in the ribs. "Don't give him any ideas," she snapped.

"Ah, my little truants," said Bruit. "Stand up against the wall with your hands in the air."

Nobody was brave enough to resist, although Beatrice did flinch away when Bruit placed his measuring tape around her waist.

"He's going to strangle my tummy!" she shrieked.

"That's not a bad idea," grinned Bruit, pulling the tape measure so tight that Beatrice began to cry. "Relax, brat. I'm just taking your measurements. El Gran Inquisitor wants me to make you a nice new outfit."

"Oh, goody!" squealed Beatrice. "Can mine be in green? Or purple? Anything but yellow or orange. I don't like yellow and orange. But I love blue and green and purple and cerise and magenta and violet. The dress I'm wearing is blue and it's very pretty, but I feel like a change. Do you like my dress, Dr. Bruit? We stole it, and after, Katey shot a seagull and a man. I don't think that was very nice do you? The seagull never hurt her. The seagull never hurt anybody. Well, he might have hurt some fish. Because seagulls eat fish. But that's not really their fault. They can't..."

"SHUT UP!!!" yelled Bruit, Katey, Sam, Jolly Roger and the rest of the prisoners. This was a mistake because Beatrice didn't like being yelled at and burst into tears.

Bruit thought about giving her something to really cry about, but decided against it. He had a lot of shifts to make and El Gran Inquisitor did not suffer delays to his execution programme lightly. Showing remarkable patience, he produced a slightly furry lollipop from his jacket pocket and plopped it in the little girl's mouth while he continued to take her measurements.

"Can I have a lollipop too?" asked Chuffy Chuck, a small boy with a large appetite and little to say for himself.

Bruit replied with a back-handed slap in the chops that left Chuffy Chuck sucking on loose teeth rather than lollipops.

At last, Bruit's work was done and his former pupils were all dressed in their brand new beige shifts. All that is except Beatrice, who refused point blank to wear it.

"Beige? Beige? There is no way I want to be seen dead in beige. It's even worse than yellow and orange. Make me a new one."

"You'll wear what you're given," snarled Bruit.

"Or what?" sniffed Beatrice. "You're already going to torture and execute us. There's nothing you can do."

Bruit turned his gaze towards Licky the dog, who had also been presented with a beige shift, and who unlike his owner seemed quite happy to wear it. Bruit picked the little dog up and cradled him in his arms.

"Nooooo!" wailed Beatrice. "Don't hurt him."

"I wasn't going to," said Bruit, taken aback. Whilst it is true that Dr. Bruit was a foul, cruel man with few redeeming points to his character, it has to be said that he was rather fond of dogs. True, he preferred large, fierce, bloodthirsty hounds to little terriers, but in general he had a soft spot for all members of the canine species, indeed he had even been known to stroke a poodle on occasion. "I was going to say, that if you wear the shift, like a good little heretic, I'll adopt this beast myself and see that he's raised good and proper. I might even let him chew on your bones if there's anything left of you after the fire's done its business."

Licky turned his little head and gave Dr. Bruit a big sloppy lick on the nose.

"Really?" said Beatrice, through her tears.

"Cross my heart."

Beatrice thought for a moment. "Well, Licky does seem to like you."

"Course he does," laughed Bruit, fondling the dog's ears. "I'll teach him to hunt and to kill and to..."

Beatrice took the shift.

"There's a good girl," said Bruit. "I'll take good care of him. You have my word."

**

Now dressed in their fine new itchy shifts, the children were escorted back to their cell and told to occupy themselves with thoughts of death because they would be put to death at first light in the morning.

"Oh good," laughed Roger. "I always find it's nice to have something to look forward to, don't you?"

"Stop blethering on," said Sam. "I'm trying to think of a way to escape."

Katey looked around the cramped cell with the tiny window. "Good luck with that. If you ask me, you'd be better off relaxing. Our goose is cooked and there's nothing we can do about it."

"I don't like this shift," sighed Beatrice. "They could have made them in green, couldn't they? They're just being mean and nasty."

"Yeah," said Chuffy Chuck, the greedy quiet kid. "I wonder what they'll give us for our last meal? They say condemned prisoners get to eat whatever they want."

"I think that only goes for murderers and the like," said Davey Jones, who liked to pretend that he knew about such things. "It's different for heretics. They usually give them a bit of bread if they're lucky."

"Rubbish," snorted Katey. "Why would they do that?"

"Oh, they say it's for our own good," said Davey. "It's coz they want us to be spiritually hungry for salvation."

"Oh. I suppose that makes sense," agreed Katey.

"No it doesn't," sobbed Chuffy Chuck. "I could eat lots and still be hungry for salvation."

"Me too," chuckled Roger.

It was then that the cell door opened and in came two young lads bearing a jug of water and a loaf of bread.

"Here you go, don't eat it all at once," said one of the lads, as they placed the food and drink on the floor of the cell. As they turned to leave, they stopped and stared at the prisoners.

"Blimey," said one.

"Stone me," said the other.

"Ron?" said Sam.

"Reg?" said Katey.

Sam and Katey were right. Their jailers were in fact, their former classmates, Ron and Reg, the cockney twins who had last been seen escaping across the moorland at Brakem Hall.

"Small world, innit, Ron?" said Reg, grinning at his old friends.

"Too right, Reg," agreed Ron.

"Aren't you dead?" asked Beatrice. "Didn't you get eaten up by Dr. Bruit's hounds?"

Reg looked down at himself to check that he was in fact alive and uneaten and then laughed. "Nope. We're alive, alright, ain't that right, Ron."

Ron nodded his agreement. "Yeah. We covered ourselves in pig poo to throw the dogs off our scent and then walked to London."

"But what are you doing here?" asked Katey.

Ron looked at his brother and winked. "Should we tell 'em?"

"Yeah, but we'll have to swear 'em to secrecy."

"For heaven's sake," sighed Sam. "They're gonna execute us in the morning. Who're we going to tell?"

"He's got a good point, Ron," said Reg.

"A very good point, Reg," agreed Ron.

"Right, it's like this, right," began Reg, lowering his voice. "We got jobs here, feedin' prisoners an' sweeping up heads after beheadings and stuff."

"It ain't as easy as it sounds, is it, Reg?" said Ron.

"Nah. There's a lot of prisoners, an' a lot of heads. Especially since the King came back an' started wearin' that stupid baked spud on his right said Fred."

"Eh?" asked Sam. "Can you say that again, in English?"

Reg laughed. "Rhymin' slang. Baked spud, hood, right said Fred, head. Get it?"

Sam nodded wearily. "Yeah. I get it. I just don't understand why you don't just say hood and head."

Ron and Reg gave each other a look and tutted. "Cos then people'd know what we were sayin', duhhhh."

"Oh, right. Carry on then," sighed Sam.

"Well, everyone thinks we're just servants right? Lowest of the low, yeah?" said Ron.

"So, isn't that what you are?" asked Beatrice.

159

"No," said Ron. "Well, yeah.... and no."

"What Ron means is... we're not what we appear to be. Ain't that right, Ron?" said Reg.

"Too right. Sound as a pound. We're really casing the joint."

"Eh? What for?" asked Sam.

"We've got the keys to every room in the place," explained Ron. "And we're gonna pinch the crown jewels."

"But don't tell anyone," said Reg.

"We won't," promised Sam.

A bell chimed mournfully in the distance.

"Twelve o'clock," said Ron. "We better get going. Nice seein' you all again."

"Yeah. Good luck tomorrow," said Reg. "Wiv the whole gettin' burned at the stake lark. They say it ain't as bad as it looks."

"It is," said Sam.

"It's worse," laughed Roger. "We've already done it, several times."

"Oh. Ah well. Never mind. Can't be helped," said Reg.

The twins were about to leave when Sam stopped them. "Hey, lads, I don't suppose you could do us a favour?"

Ron looked at Reg and then nodded. "Yeah. Anyfink for an old mate. Go on, what d'yer want? Fags? Grog? Some dirty pictures?"

"No, nothing like that," said Sam. "I was wondering if you had any spare keys you could give us? So we could get out of here?"

Reg and Ron thought about it for a moment. "What do you think, Ron?"

"I dunno. What do you think, Reg?"

160

"We was gonna pinch the jewels tonight and scarper. I don't suppose it would hurt."

"I've got a spare set of keys," said Reg.

"But they was for use in an emergency," said Ron.

"Er... hello? We're getting executed in the morning, it is an emergency," said Katey.

"Girl's got a good point, Reg," said Ron.

"Yeah. Always did have a good head on her shoulders, that one, didn't she Reg?" said Ron.

"Yeah. So, what do you think?" said Reg.

"Might as well, eh?" said Ron.

Reg handed a bunch of keys to Sam. "Here you go. There's keys to every room in the Tower."

Sam reached for the keys. "Thanks, lads. We won't forget this."

"See that you don't," said Ron. "You owe us."

"Big time," said Reg.

The twins left, locking the cell door behind them.

"Well," said Sam. "That was a turn up, eh? When do we make a break for it?"

"Give it an hour or two," said Katey. "Wait til they think we're all asleep."

"What do you mean?" asked Beatrice. "You can't possibly be thinking of escaping in these clothes can you?" She held up the shift, a disdainful sneer upon her unhappy face.

Sam jingled the keys in front of her. "We've got the keys to every room in the tower. We can raid the wardrobe room if it makes you feel happier."

Beatrice's eyes lit up. "Oooh! Really? Do they have a wardrobe room, here? I bet it's full of lovely gowns fit for a Queen. Did you know they kept Queen Elizabeth prisoner here once? And Lady Jane Grey and Anne

Boleyn. I wonder if they've kept any of their dresses? I know they'll be a bit old-fashioned but I bet we could take them in and do something to jazz them up a little."

"Yeah," agreed Sam. "We'll be sure to do that."

CHAPTER THE TWENTY-SEVENTH
DEATH OR GLORY

The drunken couple liked a good public execution. They had been to twelve already this year. While they enjoyed a good hanging or a beheading, their favourite method of dispatch was to watch someone being burnt at the stake because it was a fairly lengthy process. Word on the street had it that there was going to be mass burnings come the new morning so the drunken couple had decided to make sure of a good viewpoint by sitting up all night in front of the performance area at the Tower of London. They had each come prepared with two 36 packs of ale which they were slurping their way through during the night.

"Shlussh urrr gerogh?" asked the one with longer hair.

"Hrrrgh klugg irnmm," answered the other one who had very few teeth and those in place were nothing worth writing home about.

"Rrrrsssshhh blrrrr demtmmm!" laughed long hair, opening another can.

They didn't notice the strange rumbling sensation from the ground beneath them.

***

Queenie, desperate to save her beloved Torres from the clutches of El Gran Inquisitor had waited until nightfall before giving the order to burrow under the River Thames and into the Tower of London.

"Hisss doesssn't get it," Hiss complained as his wife told him of the plan to rescue Torres and the children.

"It's easy, silly," said Betty. "We sirens live under the sea, yes?"

"Yessss," agreed Hiss. "Hisss getsss that bit."

"Well, we're at our strongest in the water. So, we dig a tunnel under the water that will lead us into the Tower itself. When we reach the surface, the water will flood through, giving us strength and drowning our opponents."

"Yesss, that'sss a good idea, asssss far assss it goesssss," Hiss concurred. "But won't you be drowning Torres and the childrenssss too?"

Betty shrugged. "Well, if you're so clever why don't you come up with a better idea?"

Hiss couldn't think of a better idea, and sensing that his new bride was rather sensitive about the plan he kept his peace and told her it was a great plan and he was sure they'd be able to work something out to save the children when the time came. "Let'ssss jussst wing it," he said.

"Oh, goody, my brave little Hiss," said his bride, handing him a fish bowl. "Here, you'll need this."

Hiss took it and did his best to look pleased. "Thankssss, I can't waitsss to getsss some fishiessss to put in it."

Betty laughed and gave him a quick little kiss on the top of his head. "Silly boy. It's not for fish. It's for you?"

"Eh? But Hisss issss too big for fishhhh bowl. Hisss not fit in it."

"Just your head, dear heart. The bowl is full of air. It means you can come with us under the water and help save your friends."

"Oh. Great." Hiss had never prided himself on his bravery before. Yes, he could fight like a cornered rat if and when he had to, or he could sneak up on someone from behind and stick a dagger between his ribs, but sallying forth into battle had never been one of his strong points. Even so, he knew enough about women, and sirens in particular, to realise that confessing this shortcoming would not go down well, so he held his tongue and tried his best to look thrilled to bits.

"Aren't we lucky?" said Betty. "I love a good scrap and if we get killed, at least we will die together. I couldn't ask for anything more, could you?"

Hiss could ask for plenty more, but decided against it. "No. Hisss feelssss blesssed."

"Right, come on, love's young dream," said Queenie, slithering across the deck towards the happy couple. "Time for action."

Hiss donned his fish bowl helmet and followed his wife overboard and into the murky depths of the River Thames.

***

El Gran Inquisitor was restless and worried. So far his plans had gone surprisingly well. Everybody believed that he was in fact King George, but while the real King still lived he was in danger. True enough, the King was scheduled to burn at dawn, but what if someone in the crowd recognised him? What if Torres were to put in an appearance and spoil everything? He meditated on the subject for some time.

As he meditated, he reached what he called an 'epiphany'. He came to the realisation that all the failed would-be conquerers of the past had one thing in common; instead of killing their enemies straight away, they always made the mistake of showing off, of making an example of their enemies, of revealing all their plans and then naming a time in the not too distant future for them to die. He fully understood the reasoning behind this. It was good to brag about one's superiority and cleverness and it was good to demoralise one's enemies and leave them dreading the hour of their terrible death. However, all too often one's enemies, far from becoming inert with terror became desperate and managed to escape and in most cases to kill the would-be conquerer in the process. El Gran Inquisitor came to a decision. He gave orders to bring forth Captain Murderer and Dr. Bruit.

Neither of the brothers were happy at being roused from their slumber at three in the morning. They had spent the earlier part of the night drinking and eating and both were suffering the consequences of their gluttony. Murderer was toying with the idea of killing his new master if and when the opportunity arose and Bruit was more than willing to help him.

"What is it?" asked Murderer curtly.

"You will perform the act of obeisance, *por favor*," said El Gran Inquisitor.

"Eh?"

"You will bow and kiss the holy feet," explained his master.

Murderer reached for his dagger. "Captain Murderer kisses no man's feet."

"Me neither," said Dr. Bruit, grasping the needle he used for sewing shifts.

El Gran Inquisitor sighed. He would have to do something about these two. But not yet. They were still of use to him. "Very well, we shall forego the act of obeisance. Go and prepare the false King and that pompous sailor for immediate execution."

Bruit's spirits rose. "Great. What about the kids? Shall we fetch them too?"

El Gran Inquisitor shook his head. "No. They are no threat. They shall burn in the morning as planned."

Bruit looked at his brother and shrugged. "Ah well, two's better than none."

"Aye. And when they're burned we've still got their execution to look forward to in the morning," said Murderer, who always liked to have something to look forward to.

El Gran Inquisitor clapped his hands impatiently. "Well? Enough idleness. Go fetch them. Instantly."

***

The King and Captain Righteous couldn't sleep. The fact that they had been chained to the ceiling of their cell by their feet did little to improve their comfort.

"We're going to die," sobbed the King. "That fiend is going to burn us in the morning and it's all your fault."

"With all due respect, Sire, I hardly think that's fair," protested Righteous.

"I don't give a fig about fairness," snapped the King. "You were supposed to protect me."

Righteous sobbed. His King was right. He had failed. "Well, don't give up hope. There's always Torres."

"Torres? Ha!" The King spat, but because he was hanging upside down from the ceiling, his spit fell down into his face, blackening his mood even more. "Torres is a coward and a sneak and a maniac. He left us well and truly in the lurch."

"True enough, Sire," agreed Righteous. "But whilst he is free, there is hope. Is he not after all the protector of the peasant, the helper of the helpless, the love of all *señoritas*?"

"We're not peasants," snapped the King. "And we're not *señoritas*."

"Yes, but we are helpless."

"Good point," said the King. "There is that to be thankful for."

The key turned in the lock of the cell door and Captain Murderer and Dr. Bruit entered, gazing up at the two prisoners.

"You!" hissed the King. "You have some nerve showing your faces in here."

"Not really," said Murderer. "You're chained up and you're going to die. Get 'em down, brother."

Bruit pulled on a lever and lowered the two prisoners to the floor. "On your feet, dogs. It's time."

"What if I were to promise you a knighthood?" said the King.

"You can promise all you like," said Bruit. "El Gran Inquisitor has already promised to make me Duke of London."

"Yeah, and I'm gonna be the Earl of London," said Murderer, proudly.

"Just as a matter of interest, which is more important, a Duke or an Earl?" asked Righteous, dusting himself down.

"An Earl of course," said Murderer.

"No way," said Bruit. "Everyone knows a Duke is way bigger than an Earl."

"Get lost," roared Murderer. "You don't know what yer talkin' about. You tell him, Sire. You tell him who's bigger, a Duke or an Earl."

The King shrugged his shoulders. "I... I forget. Does it really matter?"

Murderer was beside himself with rage. "Does it matter? Does it matter? Of course it matt..."

Both Murderer and Bruit fell to the floor, senseless as the King and Righteous gaped at their unlikely saviours.

Jolly Roger was standing before them, laughing his head off, a heavy mace in his hand. Behind him stood Katey, Sam, Beatrice and the rest of the pirate children, armed with an impressive array of medieval swords, axes, daggers and other lethal paraphernalia, which they had looted from the Tower's arsenal.

"Bwa-ha-ha! One clunk on the head and they're off to dreamland," chuckled Roger. "I wish I could've seen their faces. That's the trouble with sneaking up on folks from behind."

"Children, release us at once," cried Righteous.

Sam fumbled with the keys to the chains but Katey stopped him.

"Not so fast, Sam," she said, her eyes aflame with anger. "I want a royal pardon first."

"Eh?" said Sam. "But he's the King. We can't make demands of a King."

"We can when he's in chains and needs our help if he's ever going to see another sunrise," said Katey.

Sam thought for a moment and then looked at the King. "Well, what about it?"

"I... but you're criminals. You sank my ship. You're pirates.... you.... I..."

"They are children, Sire," said Righteous. "Brave children at that."

"Oh, very well. Consider yourselves pardoned. Now get us out of these chains at once."

Katey smiled. "Of course, Sire."

Once they were free of their chains, the King took command. "Now, first things first, let us find some clothing suitable for a King."

"Oh, goodie!" squeeled Beatrice. "We've been looking everywhere for some nice clothes to wear but we haven't found anything yet. I hate these shifts, don't you?"

"Indeed I do," said the King.

"Is it true you have some of Anne Boleyn's old clothes here in the Tower?" asked Beatrice. "Can I have them? Can I? Can I?"

"I don't see why not," sighed the King.

"Just a minute, Sire," said Righteous. "Let's put things in perspective first, shall we? I suggest we apprehend that foul villain El Gran Inquisitor before changing our wardrobe."

"He has a good point, Sire," agreed Sam.

"No he doesn't," sulked Beatrice. "It's a stupid point."

The King was torn between his desire for vengeance and his desire to get out of his ridiculous shift. In the end the desire for vengeance won. "I'm sorry, child. Let's put El Gran Inquisitor's head on a spike first, then we'll get changed."

Beatrice thought about El Gran Inquisitor's shiny robes. "I could always make a nice frock out of El Gran Inquisitor's clothes, couldn't I?"

"By all means," said the King. "You're welcome to them."

"Then what are we waiting for?" yelled Beatrice, racing out of the cell. "Death to El Gran Inquisitor!"

CHAPTER THE TWENTY EIGHTH
FIRE! FIRE! LONDON'S BURNING!

El Gran Inquisitor waited in the Hall of Mirrors, a room, which unsurprisingly, given its name was covered wall to wall and floor to ceiling in mirrors. He admired his brand new fiery red satin robes and hood.

"I will look like an avenging angel in these robes, once the flames start to spread around the damned," he thought happily as he gave a little twirl in front of the mirrors, admiring the cut and fall of the cloth. "Guards, find out what is keeping Murderer and Bruit. Time is of the essence and I hunger to see my enemies burn."

The guards fell over themselves in their hurry to obey. They recovered their balance and opened the great doors to the Hall of Mirrors only to fall over once again as they came face to face with Jolly Roger's heavy mace.

The King and his pirate allies burst into the chamber in a fury.

"Guards! Seize them!" yelled the panic-stricken Gran Inquisitor. More guards rushed to do his bidding but fell back before the swords of the pirates and Captain Righteous. Things were looking bad for El Gran Inquisitor.

Now you have probably seen those torch things in plenty of movies about days of yore. They just sit in a holder on castle walls burning away and doing no harm. But think about it. Think what would be likely to happen if you had a blazing torch roaring away on your bedroom wall. Thought about it? Come to a conclusion? Well exactly! Those things are dangerous...and hot. And, looking on the bright side, we are happy to be able to announce that after reading all the pages in this book so far you are about to learn a moral that will help you greatly in life. Wait for it... it's coming. The King, whose eyesight was not great, decided that he would be able to see things more clearly with the help of one of those flaming torches. He reached for the handle of the torch that was burning away at the entrance to the Hall of Mirrors. The trouble is, the handle was red hot and in his shock and pain he threw it up in the air to fall against Katey's brand new shift. There's something you should know about the material those shifts were made from. It was highly flammable, for this was in the days before there were strict guidelines for children's clothing. Indeed there was a loophole specifically for shifts that were to be worn for being burnt at the stake that was still in operation up to 2011. Thankfully David Cameron, the then Prime Minister of Great Britain, finally ended this practice, thereby putting a lot of shift makers out of work. As we were saying, shifts in those days were highly flammable and in a mere moment Katey's shift had become a roaring bonfire. Sam, seeing the distress of his own true beloved, did the honourable thing and jumped on her trying to put the flames out but, to be honest, he made matters worse as his own shift created an even bigger conflagration.

"Ha! Ha! Ha!" laughed Jolly Roger. "Look at the state of them!"

"Bwa-ha-ha!" roared El Gran Inquisitor. "So burn all sinners!" He raised his sword and plunged it into Sam's back. So, before we go any further, let's go back to the moral we promised you. Never, under any circumstances play with fire while wearing a vintage shift.

But Katey was not beaten yet. As Sam died on top of her, she pulled at his burning shift and hurled it towards El Gran Inquisitor. The flaming shift caught him smack in the face and instantly he felt his gorgeous red satin hood begin to burn.

"No! He cried, pulling the hood from his head and casting it to one side. Then he and everyone else caught sight of his reflection in the mirror.... "Torres!"

Torres' pure and noble face stared back at him from the mirror. El Gran Inquisitor became enraged and attacked his own reflection. "Traitor!"

"Tyrant!" yelled his reflection.

"What's going on?" asked the King.

"Don't ask me," laughed Jolly Roger, trying without success to stop the flames that had now engulfed Katey and Sam from spreading. "I think El Gran Inquisitor and Torres must be the same person. One of those... what's the word for it?"

"Nutters?" suggested Beatrice.

"Yeah, that's it," agreed Roger. "Nutters."

The flames were spreading and King George feared that his reign was about to experience a second Great Fire of London. He watched helpless as El Gran Inquisitor fought with his own reflection. He called out his support to Torres. "Go on, son. You give him what for."

"Sire, we must flee," said Righteous, beating a path through the flames towards the door. "Come on, children. After me!"

But the inferno blocked their passage, and all being clad in highly inflammable shifts, they were all too afraid to move.

174

"It had to happen," sighed Roger. "You can only escape getting burned alive so many times."

***

Outside, the drunken couple had been joined by several other early morning sight-seers.

"What's that smell?" said one.

"Fire," said another.

"They must be havin' the executions inside," said yet another.

"That's bang out of order that is," said the first.

"What's that rumbling underground?" said another.

"Probably an earthquake," said the first, who was a bit of a know-all about such matters.

***

Back inside the burning Hall of Mirrors, things were looking bleak for everyone. Smoke and fire filled the air. And to make matters worse, that strange rumbling from underground was getting worse. Not that it seemed to be bothering El Gran Inquisitor or his reflection as they dashed through the flames cursing each other. Then, as the flames grew closer to the King and the children, the rumbling became a crescendo and a hole appeared in the mirrored floor.

"Heaven and Earth, I always knew these foundations were dodgy," complained the King.

He had no time to say anything else for at that moment a great deluge of dirty river water gushed forth from the hole in the floor, flooding the entire Hall of Mirrors.

Queenie was the first to emerge from the hole and to gaze around the flooded room. "Torres!" she called. But there was no sign of him or El Gran Inquisitor. She watched as Hiss and the rest of the sirens dragged the children, the King and Captain Righteous out to safety. "Torres, my beloved! Where are you?"

The King believed he had died and gone straight to hell when he opened his eyes and found himself lying on the damp flagstones of the courtyard outside the Hall of Mirrors, with Hiss kneeling over him, kissing his lips.

"Glak! Unhand me, beast!" he cried. "I am the King and I do not kiss monsters."

Hiss pulled away."Hisss not kisssing hisss majessssty. Hissss adminissssstering mouth to mouth rescussssscitation."

The King sat up and stared around him. A crowd of onlookers were watching as the sirens set about reviving the half drowned and half burned survivors. "What's going on?" he demanded.

"These creatures came to our rescue, Sire," said the bruised and dirty Captain Righteous.

"And El Gran Inqusitor?"

"Must have perished in the flood or the fire, Sire."

"I see. How about the kiddies?"

Righteous looked grim. "The girl, Katey and Sam... I'm afraid nothing can be done for them. The rest are fine."

The King nodded. "Well, that is something. At least."

Beatrice was crying. "Katey's dead and I was so mean to her. I kept blaming her for what she did to that seagull and... it's not fair."

"I know," chuckled Roger.

"I can't see what's so funny," said Beatrice. "Sam was your friend. So was Katey."

"I know," laughed Roger. "But did you see her face when Sam jumped on top of her? It was a classic."

***

That evening, when everyone was washed and cleaned and Katey was finally wearing one of Anne Boleyn's favourite old dresses, the King announced a banquet in honour of the fallen. The kids and the sirens stuffed themselves. The kids ate their fill of quail and roast chicken and the Sirens ate the surviving members of El Gran Inquisitor's army.

The King was happy but not content as he spoke to Captain Righteous who was seated at his right hand side. "So Bruit and Murderer escaped?"

"So it would seem, Sire," said Righteous.

"Hmmm. Well, one can't have everything, it would seem."

"Admirable sentiments, Sire," agreed Righteous.

The King turned his attentions to the children and the sirens.

"In recognition of your great service to the realm I must ask you now to keep the story of your adventures here a secret. On pain of death."

Queenie, who was mourning the loss of her beloved Torres, raised an eyebrow.

"If word got out that we had been captured by a foreign power then it would give our enemies abroad ideas. We should never be safe from copycats. The French would be sure to have a go next."

"Very well, Sire," chortled Roger. "Mum's the word."

"Good lad," said the King. "So, what are your plans?"

Roger looked at the others. "I suppose we'll set out in search of adventures and stuff. Might be a laugh."

"Oh, yes, let's go looking for treasure," said Beatrice, clapping her hands. "Then I can buy lots and lots of pretty dresses."

"Sounds like a good plan to me," said Roger. "How about the rest of you?"

"Aye aye, Cap'n," they roared.

"Captain? Me?" Roger laughed until tears ran down his cheeks.

"It's what Sam and Katey would've wanted," said Davey Jones.

"Not likely it isn't," giggled Roger. "They'd've wanted to be alive. But they haven't got much say in things anymore. Come on, lads, let's get going before the tide goes out." He turned to Hiss. "You coming with us?"

Hiss looked at the sirens. "Howsss about it girlsss? We could travel the world. Find ssssomewhere warmer than the Devil'sssss Fangssss to hang about in?"

Queenie heaved a deep sigh. "Why not? It may help me forget my beloved Torres."

CHAPTER THE TWENTY NINTH
NEW HORIZONS

And so it was that after having eaten their fill, Roger and his shipmates boarded the *Jolly Bloodbath* and prepared to say farewell to London.

"I'll miss Sam and Katey," sobbed Beatrice.

"I won't," laughed Roger. "Sam was full of himself and Katey killed seagulls."

Beatrice thought about it for a moment. "You're right. They got what they deserved, the pair of 'em. So, where next, Skipper?"

Hiss entered the cabin, holding a sheet of worn parchment in his hands. "If Hissss may make a suggessstion, Cap'n Roger?"

"By all means, Hiss," said Roger, feeling himself growing more and more pompous every time anyone called him Captain or Cap'n or Skipper.

Hiss unfolded the sheet of parchment to reveal a map. "Thissss wasss my Captain Murderer'ssss prizzzze posssessssssion."

"What is it?"

"A treasure map. It's where he buried all his lovely jewelsss and diamondssss and goldsssss."

"Yippeeee!" laughed Beatrice, clapping her hands. "What about dresses?"

Hiss shook his head. "No. Captainsssss not wear dresssessss. But you can buysss them with the jewelssss."

"Oh, yes," cried the little girl. "I like jewels almost as much as I like dresses."

"So where is this treasure, Hiss?" asked Roger.

"At the bottomsssss of the world," said Hiss.

Roger roared with laughter at this. "Bottoms! Love it. Come on then lads! We're off!"

They were just casting off when a small rowing boat pulled up alongside them. Roger peered down and saw the twins Ron and Reg, sitting in the boat.

"Permission to come aboard, Cap'n?" asked Ron.

"Permission granted," laughed Roger.

Once the twins were safely on board, Roger noted the large sacks they were carrying over their shoulder.

"What's all this, lads?" he asked.

"We'll tell him later, won't we Ron?"

"Yeah, Reg," said Ron. "We'll tell you later. Word of advice though. You better cast off quick. We might be in a spot of bother."

***

In the Tower, the King was getting ready to meet with the Prime Minister.

"It's been a while since I wore my best crown and jewels. I ought to make a show, let everyone know I'm back and I mean business," said King George to Righteous.

"An excellent idea, Sire," said Righteous who had just been promoted to Lord Admiral and was in fine spirits.

Captain Righteous accompanied his King to the Treasure House but stared in horror as they opened the doors. "Oh, no!"

The Treasure House was empty.

"Those blasted kids!" roared the King. "I'll have their heads! Righteous, commandeer the fastest ship in the fleet and bring them to me at once. I want them boiled in oil and... and everything else. I... Why did I listen to you? Why didn't I have them hung? Why? Why? It's all your fault, Righteous."

"To be fair, Sire, they did save our lives."

"Fair? Fair? I'll tell you what will be fair, Righteous. It will be fair and good and proper to see them hanging from a gibbet with their entrails hanging around their knees. Get out and do it! This instant!"

"Very well, Sire."

Not the end...

The Brothers Quinn

The Brothers Quinn are Tim Quinn and Jason Quinn. They started their writing careers as children by creating rival weekly comic books that they sold at school. Tim created 'The Banger' comic while Jason's masterpiece was a super-hero epic titled 'The Vicramer'. Film options on both still available.

Tim Quinn

After leaving school at age sixteen, Tim became a clown at the famous Blackpool Tower Circus in England. He went on to writing scripts for popular comedians of the day before entering the world of comic books in the UK on such titles as Sparky, The Topper and The Dandy. Relocating to the USA, he became the Humor Editor for the legendary Saturday Evening Post Magazine followed by a twenty year stint working for Marvel Comics on their super-hero titles. Tim has also worked in television as a producer on the award winning documentary series The South Bank Show and, with his wife Jane, run a successful management company in the music business putting on shows featuring members of Led Zeppelin and the Rolling Stones.

Jason Quinn

Jason Quinn is the award winning author of Steve Jobs/Genius by Design and Gandhi: My Life is My

Message. He has also written and edited comics for Spider-Man, Batman, Doctor Who and many more. He was both scriptwriter and script editor on the long running children's TV series Dream Street. A modern day swashbuckler, when he's not writing, eating, or reading comics, you will find him practicing his swordplay around the world as a master of the epee.

CPSIA information can be obtained
at www.ICGtesting.com
Printed in the USA
LVHW080621120822
725756LV00012B/346